$6.81

MANKILLER

Reformed mankiller Glen Lateen returned to Texas to see his ma before she died, but he hadn't even got to the family ranch when August Palau called him out. By the time the gunsmoke had cleared Palau lay dead and Glen realized that nothing had changed — in Texas the name of Glen Lateen still caused men to reach for their guns. And when murder, torture and heartache awaited him in Mora Valley, he was destined to add some more notches to his gun.

D1713247

ELLIOT LONG

MANKILLER

Complete and Unabridged

LINFORD
Leicester

First published in Great Britain in 1995 by
Robert Hale Limited
London

First Linford Edition
published 1996
by arrangement with
Robert Hale Limited
London

The right of Elliot Long to be identified as
the author of this work has been asserted by
him in accordance with the
Copyright, Designs and Patents Act, 1988

British Library CIP Data

Long, Elliot
    Mankiller.—Large print ed.—
Linford western library
    1. English fiction—20th century
    2. Large type books
    I. Title
    823.9'14 [F]

ISBN 0–7089–7949–1

Published by
F. A. Thorpe (Publishing) Ltd.
Anstey, Leicestershire

Set by Words & Graphics Ltd.
Anstey, Leicestershire
Printed and bound in Great Britain by
T. J. Press (Padstow) Ltd., Padstow, Cornwall

This book is printed on acid-free paper

1

SITTING with his back to the wall at the far right hand corner of the saloon Glen Lateen sipped his coffee slowly. Under the pale light of the kerosene lamps the kid was staring at him from the other end of the bar, near the door. He had entered a minute ago and was sampling the whisky he had ordered.

Lateen reckoned he could be no more than eighteen years of age.

And he knew the type by the arrogant lift of his thin lips, the insolent stare he had. Lateen gave an inward sigh, looked at the dregs of his coffee in the bottom of the cup. Another of them out for glory. He was sick to death of them. They gave him no peace these days.

Now the boy edged along the bar, smiling at him.

1

"I guess you're Glen Lateen," he said.

Lateen eyed him coldly. "What if it turns out I ain't? What then?"

The boy's pimply face lengthened. The sky-blue eyes hardened. "I know you are for sure, mister," he breathed.

The anger deep in him, but controlled, Lateen leaned forward, his stare baleful. "An' you've come to make yourself into a hero," he said. "That it?"

Lateen knew he was being cynical. The years had made him so, for the whole scene unfolding here was getting to be like a recurring nightmare to him. This was the seventh time he'd played it out inside two years. Now it was getting to be happening from one stinking town to the next.

The kid said, looking affronted, "I came in here for a peaceful drink, mister. Some talk."

Lateen's laugh was harsh and without mirth. It echoed through the deathly, tense silence that had now descended on the saloon. "No you didn't, boy," he

2

said. You came in here to kill me."

The kid straightened, for the first time looking slightly unnerved by the direct answer. His right hand lowered and hovered over his Colt.

"Well, for sure, you're a mean bastard, like they say," he said. "An' because o' that, I reckon you need killin'."

"An' you're goin' to do it," Lateen said.

He grinned, but it was a tired, cadaver-like grin. He let it fade slowly until his face became dark with menace. "Let me give you some advice, boy," he said. "Go home. Forget this."

Lateen watched the kid lick his lips, look around. He looked unsure, as if not knowing quite what to do next. Then his gun arm lifted slightly but stopped as Lateen cocked the hammer of the Colt he had lined up on the kid, under the table. The metallic clicks rang out like a monotonous death toll on the drum-tight silence. The boy's face went very white and scared and

3

he froze into immobility. A tic started to twitch just below his startlingly blue right eye.

"Walk away, boy, while you can," Lateen continued quietly, confidentially, as though there was only himself and the youth in the place.

The kid stiffened, blinked his startled eyes. He flicked a brief glance around him once more, then lowered his gun arm slowly.

"As you say, Mr Lateen," he said quickly. "As you say."

Lateen watched him as he turned and began to move stiff-legged towards the batwings. Lateen thought: *Don't turn, boy. Don't turn.*

But he did — swiftly; crouching and moving sideways, his right hand coming up filled with gunmetal.

Lateen's Colt rapped twice, its barking noise smashing against the confines of the saloon walls.

The silence that followed was broken only once by a man exclaiming "God almighty!" before it went quiet again.

4

Through the acrid gunsmoke rising up from under the table, Lateen could see the boy sagging. The kid's bullets were hitting the floor near his own feet. One piece of lead blew four toes off the boy's right foot before the Colt dropped from his nerveless fingers.

Then the kid gave off a sigh, before sliding sideways and slumping against a gaming table. There he fell to the floor, rolled over and stared up. His legs trembled before they stiffened out.

With bitter anger Lateen glared into the kid's wonderful blue eyes for a moment. They gazed back at him, but were devoid of life. And Lateen could swear there seemed to be a slight look of disbelief at the back of them.

Disgusted by the waste of life Lateen wrenched his gaze away, became alert to the people in the saloon once more. He flicked his gun up above the table, moving the short muzzle in a fan-like way, aiming it at the half dozen late-nighters that were in the place.

"You saw it," he barked. "Tell it how it was."

One man nodded nervously. Sweat glistened on his red face. He licked his thick lips. He gestured with a fat paw. "Sure, Mr Lateen," he said. "Like it was. Joe allus was a wild boy. Allus figured he was good with a gun."

"You should have told him he wasn't," Lateen said.

The man sniggered, as if uncertain of how to react. He had shifty, small eyes, bright as a rat's. They darted about in their sockets, as if seeking assurance all the time. "Well, yore right I'm sure, Mr Lateen," said the man. "But Joe wasn't the listenin' kind."

Lateen rose from the table, tossed two bits for the coffee on to its small, round top. The room was so quiet after the talk he could hear the wind hissing against the warped clapboards that made up the outside of the building.

Then, from the corner of his eyes, Lateen saw the barman move his hands

6

towards the underside of the counter. Lateen thumbed the hammer again. It double-clicked with loud sound in the taut silence. He straightened his arm, pointed the gun straight at the 'keep.

"Where I can see them," he demanded harshly.

The hands came up again — fast, as though jerked by strings.

"Jus — just reachin' a glass, Mr Lateen," quavered the thin, balding man.

Lateen nodded grimly. "Sure you were," he said.

His grey-blue stare looked deathly and forbidding as it searched the dim interior of this two-bit town's one saloon. He thought he would have been unknown here; thought he would have been able to rest up for a few days. But there was always one bastard that knew the legendary Texas mankiller — Glen Lateen. And there was always one bastard that wanted to topple that legend to assume his mantle . . .

He moved down the long mahogany

bar, his gun still trained on the late-night drinkers. "No silly moves, gents," he said.

Without looking at it he stepped over the body of the dead boy, edged towards the batwing doors and stared out briefly. The street was deserted, though he could see one or two lights were beginning to appear in windows. One window slid open. A man's head poked out. He peered into the street. "What's all the noise about?" he demanded.

But there was still nobody on the street to answer him. Seeing it was clear Lateen slipped through the batwings and walked swiftly up the main drag, keeping in the shadows, heading towards the livery barn, loading the empty chambers of his Colt as he went.

He was tightening the cinch on his big bay gelding when he heard the noise of men — a lot of men — coming down the street.

It hadn't taken them long, he thought

grimly. It would be the judge and jury of this town, marching towards him, he reckoned. And they would be carrying a judgement on the supposed crime he had just committed . . . a lynch rope. He had killed their blue-eyed local hero. It was time for justice to be done . . .

With grim urgency he climbed up. As he did the hostler came out of his little office, rubbing his eyes.

"What the hell's goin' on?" he demanded. "Hey, where you takin' that horse?"

Lateen rapped harshly, "Get back inside your office, man, if you want to stay alive."

With that Lateen nudged the bay forward and kicked open the big door which surprisingly swung easily on well-greased hinges. Outside it was deep dark, the sky full of cloud cover. The only light there was came from three torches carried by the mob bearing down on him.

Without hesitation Lateen sent three shots fizzing over their heads and there were immediate, panicked yells as they scampered for cover.

While they were doing it Lateen wheeled the big bay and put it into a flat-out gallop towards the hills north. A staccato of shots followed him, but the lead wasn't even close.

Now, with two days gone and well into the third, Lateen found himself deep into the mountains and still heading north. And as he rode he came to realize he had become a lonely and bitter man. Maybe warped a little, too, because of it. All he saw was his life in tatters around him. One time, when he had come out of the North-South war twelve years ago with only two slight wounds, he'd had high hopes.

But now . . .

What was he? A mankiller. And now, it seemed, a slaughterer of gun-crazy boys, out to acquire a reputation. Admittedly he was renowned, even feared, throughout the southwest and sought out because of that, but, in reality, nothing more than an executioner.

And he had never wanted it. It had just happened. Then, again, that wasn't exactly true, either. Since an early age he'd had this hell in him, this go-to-the-devil attitude that wouldn't take nothing from anybody, no matter how trivial. And he had become a marked man. Every gunsel in the territory wanted his hide nailed to the wall, his notch on their gun.

He stared at the blue Texas ridges reaching ever onwards ahead, toward the prairies and high country.

It was time to change. It was time to bury the past. He had to give himself one last chance . . .

2

"GLEN. There's a letter for you."

Lateen stopped his progress down the only real street Aspen Creek could boast of. He was heading towards the OK Saloon for a long, cool beer and a rare steak. He turned to find it was Cy Bains from the stage office close behind him. He was waving the missive in his hand.

"Arrived on the noon stage yesterday," Bains explained when he caught up. "Been waiting for one of the boys from the ranch to come in so's he could deliver it." He grinned. "Turns out to be you."

Lateen took the letter, his blue-grey stare studying the writing on the front of it. No doubt about it, it was his sister Helen's precise, careful hand.

It was the first communication he

had received from her in four years. She had been his only link with the family since the rancorous parting twelve years ago. And the reawakened memories the letter created — even after all this time — caused Lateen to set his chin into a grim, lean line, for they were still gut-twisting, still vivid, those memories.

And, though they were unwanted, they began to relive themselves again as he stood there.

He had been returning home — returning from the hell of the North-South conflict. But in Fort Worth he had killed a man. Though it had been self-defence they had jailed him for two months while the matter was cleared up. However he found the ungenerous press accounts of it had preceded him when he got home. He had arrived to find he had been tried and found guilty, though the Fort Worth court had fully exonerated him.

It had been a harsh, moral-toned condemnation from his mother concerning it. Always a high-nosed, bitter woman after the death of his father, she had made it clear through those years that she thought she should have had better from life than a dusty Texas range and a man who had inconsiderately died on her six years after they had settled in the Mora Valley. Even so, despite everything, Lateen recalled, she hadn't quit the place. He felt he grudgingly had to give her that. No, instead she had gone on to build herself an empire, so he'd heard. The Double L these days — he had been led to believe from accounts gleaned from railhead bars — was a brand to be reckoned with in south Texas.

But the final straw for him in the whole thing had been his brother Abel's reaction to his homecoming. Abel had gone along with Ma all the way. He had said that, choose which way you looked at it, the taking of human life was a grievous sin before God unless it happened to be for the Lord they served, or their Country, or in the Defence of Property. Abel, he

14

remembered, had put his own capitals to the last part.

Now, feeling the mid-summer Wyoming sun hot upon him Lateen hauled back from his memory and compressed his thin lips. Even now, he still found a certain hypocrisy in Abel's self-righteousness. He had expected better from a man who had seen something of life and had had his left foot blown off at Antietam, ending, what had been for him, a bravely fought war.

Lateen admitted to himself that he had been outraged by his homecoming. And that he had quit his family in disgust, leaving them to their piety, even though he'd had the feeling — and his sister Helen had agreed with him, stood by him and taken his part through it all — that once they *had* vented their spleen on him they would have forgiven him and taken him to themselves again.

But, full of hell-fire and youthful indignation, he had decided they could go to devil and live in their swamp of piousness for he'd had more than enough of it. He just didn't want their condescension, or their moralising. Through the years, however, he had continued to let Helen know where to find him, just in case he was ever needed, or that Ma had changed her mind about him . . .

He stared down the busy Aspen Creek street. Heaving a sigh he dismissed his sombre thoughts. But it was with a slight tingle of excitement he tore open the envelope and scanned the contents. He was pleased to learn that Helen had at last married — to a man named Horst Blackstock — and that they had a son James, now three years old. There was more general news, then the passage that caused his gut to tighten:

Ma's dying, Glen, though, of course, she won't have it. She says she's not ready for the Lord yet. But come if you can, though I am not sure what your reception will be, or whether she will still be alive when you arrive. I

16

must warn you, though, there is still no forgiveness in her.

Lateen blinked at that and looked up. Cy Bains' enquiry near his ear was gentle, but probing. "Bad news, huh, Glen?" he said.

Lateen turned and stared at the clerk. "Not the kind you want to hear, Cy, no matter how long it's been, I guess," he said heavily.

He turned and left the stage company man gazing after him, a puzzled look on his face.

And Cy continued to stare at the tall man's broad back as it receded from him up the boardwalk.

As a small-town man Cy wanted to know more, but was too afraid to ask a man like Glen Lateen. For since he had arrived in Radiant Valley five years ago Glen had become known as the quiet man — and a hard man to get to know. And always, Cy had had this sure conviction in him that there was another very different side to Glen Lateen — a dark, cold, merciless,

17

unforgiving side. For whatever contact Cy had had with him, however trivial, he had been left with the uncomfortable feeling that to run up against Glen Lateen would be to commit yourself to some very sudden, bloody violence. Because, although Lateen came over as an apparently mild man who kept himself to himself, he seemed to carry this strange aura of menace about with him, even death.

Cy narrowed his eyes as the thoughts passed through his brain. He had to admit, it was the craziest feeling.

Unaware of Cy's thoughts, as he walked, Lateen found odd regret was seeping into him, renewed by Helen's letter. What a waste of the years it had been after that acrimonious breakup.

He set his jaw. Oh, he could have blamed his ma and Abel for it all — and did for quite some time — but after his anger and pain at being rejected and his reaction to it, there had often been remorse.

To try and salve the memories, he

stared with sober appreciation at the small town around him. The last five years here in Radiant Valley had been the first real normality he had known since he walked into hell at Gettysburg as a callow youth of sixteen.

And the survival of that savage conflict had bred a certain callousness in him, an almost reckless disregard for his own life and the lives of other men he wasn't beholden to — but to those that he was, he had a passionate loyalty and had seen many of them die.

He knew now, though, choose what the family reaction to him had been, he should have stayed at home. He should have realized Ma would certainly have had need of him, Pa being dead all those years and Abel as restricted as a hobbled stallion since he had come home with his foot blown off. Maybe if he had done that, his life would have never come to what it did.

But he hadn't. Instead, like a lot of Johnny Rebs embittered by defeat, and in his case burdened with the further indignity of being censured by his own family, he had turned to hell-raising.

And from that point on it had been cattle trails, gunfights, rotgut whisky, gambling — but for one brief, odd perversity for a Texas cowboy. He'd tried a spell at being a trailtown Kansas lawman until he'd had to call out a prominent townsman for dealing a crooked deck to wet-eared Lone Star cowpokes. The outcome of that was to be accused of still being Southern trash and asked to turn in his badge and leave town quickly . . . while his neck was still the same length.

Yes, he knew he had been a brash young Reb with a chip on his shoulder the size of a log. And inevitably, with years of deadly gunplay behind him, gunsels hearing the name of the man they had come up against was Glen Lateen had blanched and some had revealed their more discretionary nature and declined to take the matter further. Those that hadn't, had died. But later, when his reputation had grown so strong, there had been the kids . . . and that had been something else.

He had become sickened by it. He'd found with his go-to-hell ways he had triggered himself into a corner. The end of which, for him, would inevitably be looking at some sonofabitch who was faster than he was — and had the nerve to back it up — through the last gunsmoke he was ever going to see. There had even been one time, he thought with bitter regret, when he'd hired out his gun for money . . .

Then had come that lonely night in that no-account backwater town when the last of the wide-eyed kids had called him out. He had decided the boy had been one killing too many and he had rode into the brasada that Texas night, not heeding the thorns that tore at his chaperos, vowing never to live by his gun again . . .

Now he was foreman for the Iron Fork — a medium-sized spread in this high, but sheltered and remote valley in Wyoming territory owned by John

Gullet, an able and kindly man. And Lateen admitted that over the past few years he had become the nondescript he had grown to want to be — the gunsmoke blown away and all the hell he'd had in him drained out to leave what he hoped was the true man.

He allowed the memories to fade again. With a grunt he forgot the beer and steak he had been heading for and turned back to the wagon parked outside George Bailey's General Store.

He found the monthly ranch order he had come into town for was being loaded by George's two strapping sons. When he walked into the store out of the heat Bailey looked up from his books and gave him a puzzled frown. "You're back early, Glen," he grunted. "Beer gone flat?"

Lateen stretched his hard, lean face with a grim smile. "I'd appreciate it if you'd load the wagon quick as you can, George."

At that Bailey narrowed his gaze,

looked both interested and surprised. "Trouble?"

Lateen pursed his thin lips. He felt he should say something but found he was still reluctant to discuss his affairs after all the on-the-edge trails he'd ridden when one slip of the tongue could have proved fatal. Even the recent five years of ranching domesticity and good neighbourliness hadn't softened the trait that had matured in him over the formative and violent years.

"Just a family matter," he offered.

Bailey nodded understandingly, knowing Lateen's penchant for taciturnity. "Sure Glen," he said. He picked up Lateen's list and scanned it. "I'll get the boys to hurry it up."

A quarter of an hour later Lateen urged the team out of Aspen Creek, the high-sided wagon — piled with goods and spares for the ranch — roped down. He went through Benn's Cut and followed the stream on to the rolling meadowlands of the Iron Fork range.

An hour later John Gullet met him on the worn ground before the modest ranchhouse, built in the shade of the cottonwoods standing in graceful ranks along the creek. Faint surprise was on Gullet's lined face to see him.

"You're back early, Glen," he said. "I said you needn't rush. Nothin' spoilin'."

"I'll take what pay's due to me, John," Lateen said abruptly.

The rancher's long face lengthened more. Puzzlement furrowed his narrow brow. "Hell, what's that supposed to mean?" he demanded.

Lateen eyed the tall, spare man before him. He knew Gullet's history, for the rancher had told it to him almost straight off so — as the man had said — there would be no illusions or surprises. Gullet had told him he was a former Federal captain, and without modesty, had said that he had served with distinction and had the medals and scars to prove it. Even faced with such frankness Lateen found his

24

taciturn nature would not allow himself to go into such detail. But he had volunteered his own mankiller name out of cussedness, or pride. Gullet hadn't flinched. He said he had heard of it in the Kansas cowtowns, but as far as he knew Glen Lateen wasn't a name known around Radiant Valley or Wyoming. And, he'd said, it wouldn't matter to him anyway. That past was for Texas to worry about.

Instead Gullet had gone on to say, "You say you've punched cows. That bein' so I'll judge you on that, and not what's gone before." Gullet's narrow appraisal had then been long and hard. "And whose side you were on during that damned war don't matter a hoot to me, either. We all lived our piece of hell in those years."

So the outcome had been, three years later, that Gullet had made him his foreman.

Lateen drew himself up. He just couldn't be brief with the man who had befriended him when most men would have turned him away. And by now Gullet knew most of Lateen's own background history too, leaked over applejack on cool summer evenings rocking on the stoop.

So he said, "Ma's dyin', John. I have to go, make my peace."

Gullet sighed, looked hesitant for a moment, before nodding. "Yeah . . . well, I guess you do." The rancher's grey eyes narrowed as he stared at him imploringly. "But you'll be comin' back, won't you son?" he said quickly. "I want that. An' Mary'll take it bad if you don't."

Here Gullet paused, rubbed his bushy sideburns and looked side-wise at him. The tall, spare rancher even looked uncomfortable, which, Lateen decided, wasn't in character at all. "An' well, damn it," the old man went on, "the thing is I'm not gettin' any younger. I'd like to see the ranch — *an'* Mary — left in good hands before I go . . . yours."

Slightly shocked Lateen eyed the tall, grey-haired man. He hadn't fully realized John had known there was something deep growing between himself and Mary. Nor that the rancher was thinking in terms of marriage between them. And, John Gullet's spoken intention of leaving the ranch to him, was an even bigger surprise. But maybe he was being naive, Lateen thought. He knew he could be — for, thinking back, Gullet had dropped enough hints about him and Mary.

"You don't mind 'bout me sparkin' Mary, then?" he said.

Gullet shook his head vigorously. "Hell, no," he said. "I thought I'd been makin' that plain, in a roundabout way for some time. You've growed to be a fine man, Glen." He nodded fervently. "An' if *you* don't know it, I do. You used your head when the blood cooled. You got the hell out of your system an' settled before it was too late. A lot of men never do that."

Lateen began to feel a deep peace fill him and an even greater respect than he already had grow in him for this tall, lean man before him. Gullet had never judged him; had accepted him as he had found him. Now he was saying he didn't mind an ex-hellraiser and mankiller marrying his daughter.

It prompted Lateen, with a rare impulsiveness, to put out his hand. "I'll be back, John," he said. "By God, you have my solemn word on that."

Gullet took his gnarled mitt warmly. "An' that's all I need," he said. "Now go an' find Mary and say your farewells, though I guess *that* won't be as easy as this."

3

AND it hadn't been easy explaining his need to go to Mary, but eventually she had understood and had given him her blessing and her love. Now, six weeks later and sore from long hours in saddle, Lateen came down out of the high country and into the East Mora Valley.

He was glad for the warmer feel to the air as he eased the big roan and pack mule through the familiar foothills of the land he had grown up in.

But at Fisher's Creek — the stream that had cut a small, high valley out of the northern foothills — the thick column of smoke rising into the blue sky caused him to pull rein and chew his bottom lip thoughtfully as he gazed at it. He should ride on, he mused, for whatever it was, it could be none of his business. But there was more

29

smoke there than would be emitted from an ordinary homestead chimney stack, or pile of burning trash, that much he knew.

So it was with an odd feeling of wary anxiety he turned the roan and headed towards it. After a three mile ride along a well-used trail, with sheep grazing amongst the clumps of brush each side, he found the sod building — erected against a gaunt, brown bluff. The roof, he could see, was caved in. The timbers that had supported it still smouldering.

Whatever had happened here, he reckoned, had happened within an hour or so. The outbuildings, too, he observed, were gaunt and fire-wrecked.

Then he saw the woman. She was sitting spread-legged against the corral fence — the only thing that hadn't been destroyed here. What horses had been in there had gone. Lateen could see the woman was blank-eyed and shocked, her face bruised. A little girl of maybe three years of age was sitting with her, clinging to the woman's dust-soiled skirts. The button was hugging a rag doll as well, her dark eyes round, frightened pools that were lifted up, gazing at him.

Then, to his left, on the edge of a copse of cottonwoods about thirty yards away Lateen saw the man hanging. His face was purple and bloated through strangulation, his tongue lolling out. He was swinging in the slight breeze that funnelled up this narrow valley. Lateen wondered how long it had taken the poor bastard to die, for the rope had clearly not broken his neck.

Then he heard the sound of a bullet being jacked into the breech of a rifle . . . behind him.

Tensing up he raised his hands. "Now easy," he said softly. "I'm turnin'. There'll be no tricks."

"As you said: easy. No tricks." The suggestion, Lateen judged, was from a boy whose voice was on the break.

When he saw him Lateen guessed the lad was maybe fourteen years of age.

He was tall for his age, his face spotted with acne. The rifle in his hands was held firm and steady, though, and was trained on his midriff. Lateen pretended to ignore the weapon, but felt the boy could use it if the need arose.

"What's your name, boy?" he said.

The youth seemed slightly surprised by the question and Lateen's apparent disinterest in the weapon pointing at him. It suggested to Lateen that the boy had expected something more.

"Abe Wayne," he said, "if it's any of your business."

Lateen nodded towards the cadaver on the end of the rope. "Kin of yourn, son?"

He saw the boy's hands tighten reactively on the rifle, his lips clamp into a thin line. He said, "My pa."

"I see," Lateen said.

Lateen stared at the boy. The kid was having one hell of a job to remain brave.

"Five men came," the kid blurted

then, his voice high-pitched, as though he was getting desperate to tell somebody, get some urgent support for his pain. "They claimed Pa was stealin' Double L cattle. They had Double L hides over their saddles, sayin' it was proof we had — "

"Double L, you say?" Lateen cut in sharply. *The family ranch?*

The boy nodded. Lateen saw his gaze was imploring as it met his own level stare. "They said they'd found the hides in the open-sided shack we have a mile down the crick," the kid went on, his voice rising another tone. "We use it for the spring shearing."

Now Lateen saw tears begin to well up into the boy's eyes; saw his lower lip tremble. "They're damned liars, sir," he shouted, his misery starting to thicken his voice. "Would we be fool enough to leave them there, if we had . . . ?"

Lateen shook his head, narrowed his eyelids. "No, boy, I don't think you would," he said, "not if you've any damned sense. But I find it hard to believe the owners of the Double L ordered this."

He waved his arm around at the charred wreckage, the hanging man.

At the hinted defence of the Double L the boy's tear-filled gaze darted up again, animal aware. A haze of fear and suspicion shadowed their greyness as Lateen held the gaze. Then the boy squared his shoulders and set his chin. He made a tighter grip on the rifle.

He demanded, "You one of them?"

Lateen nodded. Maybe he should lie, he thought. But he didn't.

"I'm kin, boy," he admitted, "but that's as far as it goes. Did you see the men's faces, or know them?"

"Kin?" the boy's eyes rounded. "You kin?"

Despite his clear shock and a moment's unsureness the boy shook his head, looked, for some reason, as though he wanted to trust him and Lateen felt himself relax slightly and feel thankful for that.

"They had hoods over their heads and rode unbranded horses," the boy went on. Then he stared, narrowly, as if still not certain. "I know all the Lateens," he said suspiciously. "But I ain't seen you around."

Lateen tightened his lips. He could go into a full explanation. Instead he nodded towards the ghastly cadaver, swinging from the tree.

"What you aim to do with your pa, boy?" he said. "Bury him? I can help."

At that the sound of the woman's voice, harsh and ringing, came from the corral rails.

"He stays where he is until Barret Tucker's seen him."

Lateen turned and looked at her. He found she was staring coldly up at him, clearly fighting her way out of her shock. Her pale, dirt-smeared face was bruised and was set into severe lines. Her grey eyes were dark-ringed and sunken. They were boring into his gaze, the deadness he had first seen in them gone to leave blazing defiance.

"He the law?" Lateen said.

"Craddock's town marshal."

"He won't have any jurisdiction here, ma'am," Lateen said. "Needs U.S., or county law for somethin' like this."

"He's the on'y law we have close," the woman said. "An' the county law is in the Double L's pocket."

Lateen's ears pricked up. "You sayin' the law's corrupt?"

The woman nodded. "If that's the word."

With a grunt of pain she got up and Lateen didn't pursue the topic further. The child still clung tightly to her skirts and was dragged up with her. Lateen found the button's eyes were continuing to gaze fixedly at him, bright fear and bewilderment at the back of them. God knew what she had witnessed here, Lateen thought.

"So, what are you aimin' to do, ma'am?" he said. "I mean your circumstances bein' what they are."

"What's it to you if you are what you say you are — a Lateen?" She spat out the name with harsh, loathing venom.

Lateen pursed his lips. He said, "Ma'am, God's truth, I wouldn't be party to this."

The woman glared at him before turning her eyes to the boy. "Abe's strong," she said. "He's the man here now." But when she swung her gaze back, it was slightly incredulous, as though she hadn't fully comprehended what had gone before. She demanded, "You actually claim to be kin to the scum that did this and can stand there? I just can't believe you could have the gall." She turned abruptly and called, "Abe, hold that gun real straight on him!"

—As if galvanised the boy tightened his grip on the rifle. Lateen could see he held it with confidence, though tears still dampened his acne'd face. And in his eyes Lateen could still see the remnants of young innocence, though he figured this harsh country would soon erase that.

"Now, just tell me who you really are, mister?" the woman demanded.

Even with that big bore staring at him Lateen saw no point in lying. He had already committed himself. He found he was appalled that the Lateen name could be attached to this. It really didn't fit with Ma, Abel and Helen at all. Something drastic must have altered them.

Lateen stared down at the family from the saddle. "I'm Glen Lateen, ma'am," he said.

The woman's eyes narrowed before they widened again, as if recalling some long buried memory. "The mankiller?" she breathed. She added harshly, "Rumour was you were good riddance dead." Then scorn filled her voice. "You come back to add your gun to that devil's brood already nesting on the East Mora?"

Lateen held her gaze, his own as steady and honest as he could make it.

"No, ma'am," he said. "That's not why I'm here at all. You've got to believe that."

"Believe a killer, name of Lateen?" The woman made a disparaging noise and spat phlegm to the hard-packed earth. Then she stared around her, her face taking on a tragic aspect as her bony right hand went tremblingly up to her mouth. She looked on the point of breaking down, but Lateen knew she wouldn't.

"Look what your scum have done to me," she shrilled. "I'd rather believe a drunken Comanche than any of your clan. Now go before I ask the boy to do somethin' I'll maybe regret. Leave me and mine to our grievin'."

Respect filled Lateen. The woman was steel-hard, strong enough to hold off what must be a blistering need for revenge. He judged from his years living with John Gullet and absorbing his philosophy on life gained through his book learning, she was filled with just the type of raw honesty and guts he knew was needed to settle and build this land. Though her husband's corpse was swinging in the breeze not thirty yards from where they stood, the rope creaking as it rubbed against the limb of the cottonwood it was slung over, yet she was standing there snarling her she-cat defiance. But she was also right-minded enough to be willing to allow the law to arbitrate on this atrocity, though it was her husband swinging there and himself a member of the family strongly suspected as having committed it.

That took something special in Texas, he decided. Maybe, while he'd been away, the state had done some growing. For, yes, this woman represented something solid. She was not a drifter, a gunslinger, a cow puncher, or one of the long riding scum still crawling over the west, killing and looting. No, she was of the small, hard core that was moving in to settle and nourish this land. A proud woman filled with a dogged determination to go on, no matter what, to make her mark. She was like John Gullet, he thought. She could have told the boy to shoot him though, but no, she hadn't.

He nodded his head, touched his dirty, sweat-greased low-crowned stetson. "As you wish, ma'am. I'll tell the marshal you need him here."

4

AN hour and a half later Lateen paused on the last rise overlooking the township of Craddock. He surveyed the spread of buildings before him with narrow eyes. The town had grown since the last time he had seen it. Then, all there had been were a merchantile, ten adobe buildings, a livery barn plus smithy and a range full of maverick longhorns.

At the building that announced it was the marshal's office he climbed down, tied up the pack mule and roan. He found the door was locked. He stopped a passerby.

"You know the whereabouts of the marshal?" he said.

"Out on the range, every Tuesday an' Thursday, practisin' with his rifle," the man replied.

Lateen nodded. "Obliged. Afore you

go, mister, if you do see the marshal, tell him I found a man hanging from a tree at the Wayne place, up on Fisher Creek. They're burnt out, too. I promised Miz Wayne I'd pass the word on. But I may be gone by the time the marshal gets back."

At the news the man stared, his eyes rounding and bulging. "You found Jim Wayne hangin'?" he blurted. "Gawd a'mighty. What about Nellie, Abe an' the yonker?"

Nellie? Lateen thought. Wayne's wife?

"Bad shaken, I'd say, but OK," he said. "I wanted them to come in but they wouldn't. Said they'd wait for Tucker to go out there." He climbed up into his saddle again. "You do that?"

The man nodded. "Sure. Sure. Who are you, mister?"

"If need be, I can be found at the Double L."

The man's eyes narrowed. "The Lateen spread?"

43

Glen nodded. "Unless it's changed hands."

The passerby shook his head fiercely. "No, no," he said. "Still the Lateen spread." The man switched his gaze meaningly to the Colt at Lateen's hip, nestled in the well-oiled holster. "You wouldn't be goin' to work for them, would you?"

But Lateen ignored the question. He took the pack mule's lead rope and when mounted he pulled the roan round and headed off down the street, feeling hot and sweaty under the frying early afternoon sun. He decided on a beer and whisky to chase it before he stirred more trail dust for the family home. After what he'd found at the Wayne place, he decided he needed it.

At the Schooner Saloon tie-rail he secured the roan and pack mule again. A cautious glance around told him Craddock had grown to be a typical, busy range town. One street, fronted with wooden business premises, though some — such as the bank and jail — were now of brick.

But on the rising ground lifting away from the river, whose big bend held the town to its loop, there was a mix of imposing adobe and clapboard houses taking the more prosperous populace away from, Lateen suspected, the strong odours and noise of the town.

Inside the saloon Lateen ordered the beer and whisky. A sip told him the ale was good and thankful for that he took a long swallow to swill down the Texas dust, feeling his tiredness slowly begin to drain out of him. Then he dropped the whisky in one. It had been a long, hard trail from Radiant Valley, Wyoming. And the gruesome find at Fisher's Creek hadn't helped. God help Missus Wayne and her young.

But the voice from behind set the skin on his back crawling. "By God," it said. "Glen Lateen. Rumour had it you were daid."

Funny thing . . . rumour, Lateen thought cynically. Rumour had had him dead umpteen times. He turned.

He didn't like voices coming from behind him. It had always led to all sorts of things in the past, usually bad.

He levelled his steady gaze on the owner of the voice. The man was rising from the card table nearby. Lateen could see he was of medium height. His thin smile gashed his dark, stubbled chin. And it was . . . Lateen blinked. *Rafe Palau?* Hell, he'd thought that had been all over, years ago . . .

Lateen watched Palau straighten to his runt height, grinning. Palau's eyes already glittered death, but the mirthless smile Lateen remembered Palau always wore was still there.

"I suppose," Palau said in a slow drawl, "it would be too much to ask for us to shake hands?"

Lateen didn't miss the faint mockery that was at the back of the voice. And disconcertingly Lateen found himself taking too much time to adjust to the knife-edge co-ordination of brain and muscle he knew he must have if he was to survive the next few moments. For, no doubt, Palau was out to kill him. It had been a long time since Lateen had drawn his gun to defend himself, though he had practised on cans weekly . . .

He nodded. "Right," he agreed. "I'd sooner shake hands with a skunk."

The remark brought ugly resentment to Palau's face, wiping away the toothy grin. He rubbed his gun hand nervously on his shirt. It was as though it had suddenly got slightly damp with sweat.

"Your mouth always was too big," Palau breathed. "And I suppose it would be too much to ask you if you are here on business . . . ?"

Lateen nodded again. "It would," he said.

Palau spat sidewise into the brass cuspidor close by. "Well, we never did finish that business in Dodge, did we?"

Lateen felt his body was slowly settling in to the cold calm of years ago, the edginess in it gone now he knew for sure what was to be demanded of him here.

He said, "I thought I had."

Deliberately, watchfully, Lateen studied the man before him. "I put four bullets into you, Palau," he went on. "Most men would have figured that enough. But the devil looks to his own, I guess."

At that slow, almost arrogant retort, Palau scowled, his yellow-brown eyes flashing momentarily. "And that includes you, Lateen," he breathed. "The devil has looked after you most of all."

For the first time Lateen allowed a thin, mirthless smile to flicker across his lean features. He spread his hands apart mockingly, the beer mug still held loosely in his left hand. "Well, if that's all, Palau," he said, "I'll get to my drinking again."

With a growl Palau straightened and reared up to his full five feet four inches. His lips twisted into a snarl. He rasped, "Not in a coon's age, it ain't all."

Lateen's blue-grey eyes turned bleak. He didn't want this, didn't need it. All this had been put behind him, years ago. He wanted like hell for it to stay there. Irritated by the turn of events he set his lean jaw.

"I'm passin' through, Palau," he said with quiet warning. "Be content with that. I'm not lookin' for trouble here."

"Content, hell!" Palau barked. He crouched, his facial colour draining, leaving it pale and gaunt. "You damn near blew me apart back there in Dodge. I was six months healin'." Palau moved his hand towards his Colt. "But you won't take the edge this time, Lateen."

At that the startled, uncertain men around Lateen and Palau rose or moved hurriedly to get out of the firing line, sending chairs skittering back in their mad scramble.

Lateen didn't seem to move, apart from raising his right shoulder slightly. The roar of the two guns mingled,

49

battering their noise against the saloon walls. Then the room went quiet again. Only acrid gunsmoke drifted in the still air.

Palau was sagging, glaring bug-eyed through the gunsmoke at Lateen. Blood was seeping through his grey shirt front; trickling down his chin. He appeared to be attempting to mouth something, but no sound was coming out of the thin lips, only the crimson gore.

As he teetered Palau tried to raise his gun once more but it seemed too heavy to lift. But he managed to fire it. Its discharged bullet ploughed across the floorboards sending a dirty brass cuspidor clattering through the batwings into the street.

Lateen glared through the gunsmoke. He found that he had no mercy in him for Palau, and that the shawl of respectability he had cultured over the past five years in Radiant Valley had dropped away as though it had never existed. He was a mankiller again.

Grim-faced and deliberate, he drove

his third bullet clean through Palau's brain. There wouldn't be a third time for Palau, he resolved savagely. That bastard had dealt his last card.

The impact of the lead stamped a half inch hole in Palau's forehead sending him staggering back through the chairs and tables to flatten against the side wall of the saloon before slithering down it, his dead eyes staring at nothing, his gun clattering to the floor, his blood and brains streaking the pine boards behind him.

Feeling wire-taut now, Lateen turned viciously and stared around him, hammer on the Colt thumbed back again, his lips drawn back off his strong, even teeth.

"Anyone else feel lucky?" he rasped.

But all he saw were shocked faces, hands held judiciously wide — well away from hardware. And the stunned quiet that descended in the saloon stretched until — though still clearly shaken — a big, well-dressed, bluff looking man standing nearby breathed,

"That was cold-blooded, sir."

Lateen flicked the Colt around to cover the owner of the voice. He stared at him with steely eyes. "Wrong," he grated. "That was self preservation. You got more to say?"

The stranger stared at him for moments before he turned to make for the batwing doors. With two long strides Lateen was barring his way. He grabbed the man's coat lapel and pulled him round, pushing the hot Colt barrel against the man's gullet. "You goin' somewhere?" he growled. "Maybe for friends o' his?"

Confronted so brutally the man straightened and looked angrily indignant. "The undertaker," he said. "He clearly has business here. You have seen to that." He looked at Lateen's hand on his lapel. "Now, if you will release me . . ."

Lateen narrowed eyelids, took a fresh hold. "By God, your name, mister? I'm in no mood for niceties."

The man clearly resented the hand

on his fine Prince Albert coat. "I am Horst Blackstock, of the Double L," he said heatedly. "Now, again, I ask you to take your hand off my coat."

Shock jarred Lateen. Horst Blackstock? Didn't Helen say she had married a man by that name? But there was something else about the man, he realized suddenly, shockingly. His face — though fifteen years older — he knew it. During the war. But where? Lateen racked his brain. It wouldn't come. And that hadn't been the name he had gone under . . .

"What's Palau to you?" he demanded, dismissing the flashback.

Blackstock looked at him resentfully. "He was my niece's husband."

That completely threw Lateen. He had always known Palau to be nothing more than a two-bit gambling gunslinger, stage robber and backshooting murderer. Decidedly not a family man. But then, Lateen reflected, up until five years ago he'd been no angel, either. However, for a gut-low rat like Palau to be married to Helen's husband's niece and automatically making him kin took some hard swallowing.

"Mister," he said, "I gave him more than a short chance to change his mind. He didn't."

Lateen found Blackstock returning his own stare with now steady dark eyes. He seemed to have settled down a little. "All you gave him here was death," he said in measured tones. "Now, your hand off my coat, if you please."

Uneasy, Lateen stared at his brother-in-law, finding it hard to believe Blackstock was such kin. And that feeling he had just had — the feeling he'd known, or seen, this man before and that it had been something bad — still nagged him. And there was another thing that was odd, too — Palau calling his name hadn't seemed to bring a reaction from Blackstock. But maybe he hadn't heard it . . .

Lateen allowed his hand to slide off

the quality cloth, but a whisper of anger still quibbled through him.

"You've got a fine mouth, Blackstock," he said. "But I'll tell you this — Palau was a rat who deserved to die."

The batwing doors crashing open, drowning his last words, turned Lateen's gaze off Blackstock. Framed in the doorway he saw a tall, burly man. Below the man's big nose was a bushy, walrus moustache. He held a Parker shotgun firmly in his large, bony hand. Lateen saw a star decorated his vest front. The intruder's narrow, suspicious stare found Palau first, then Blackstock. Then Lateen watched the lawman's gaze harden when he saw the Colt he had in his hand. Marshal Barret Tucker started to bring the Parker up.

Lateen felt his gut tighten. He lined up the Colt. "Man," he hissed, "I'm hot. Don't do anythin' foolish."

Barret Tucker's middle-aged, long face lengthened at the sudden, deliberate move and terse warning from Lateen. After moments of clear indecision

Tucker swung his gaze on to Blackstock. His gun remained lowered.

He said, "What happened here, Blackstock?"

The big, well-dressed man gusted heavy breath. "Well, though you can't really miss it, Barret, there has been a gun fight," he said with a faint hint of sarcasm. "And, as you can maybe also see, my nephew-in-law, August, lies dead."

Though he was still tauter than drawn-up Glidden wire, Lateen felt an odd tinge of grim humour prod him . . . *August* Palau, for God's sake? But he was soon sobered by the lawman's keen gaze as it turned on to him.

"What's your story?" Tucker demanded.

"It was him or me," he barked.

The lawman tightened his lips and looked again at Horst Blackstock. "That the way of it?"

Blackstock again gusted air, down his nostrils this time. "They appeared to know each other," he said. "They seemed to have some old, unsettled

56

score between them."

Tucker glanced at the people around him, who were now seeming to start to come down from their heights of startled tension. Some low, awed talk was even beginning to buzz.

"That the way it was?" he demanded.

Heads nodded. One man said off-handedly, "It was fair an' square, Marshal. August seemed to want it no other way. Fact was he called the play. This man — " He indicated with a grudging nod to Lateen " — wanted to leave the past buried and go on his way."

Lateen met the lawman's stare as he turned to him. It was icy cold. "What's your name, mister?" he said.

Lateen saw no point in evasion. "Glen Lateen."

The lawman's face paled. Then he said, his voice barely audible, "My God, it seems the buzzards are gatherin'."

He turned swiftly to look at Helen's husband.

"You know about this?"

Lateen became aware that Blackstock, too, was staring at him in disbelief. His brother-in-law ignored the marshal.

"Glen?" he breathed. "Helen said she'd written, but . . . "

Lateen levelled his hard gaze on him. "But what?"

Blackstock blurted, his round face reddening, "I didn't think you'd come. Nor did she. Fact is, rumour had come down to us you were dead. Her letter was purely speculative."

Lateen stared, his face grave under the grey dust and tan. "It was, huh?" he grunted.

There was a sudden rumble of concurring opinion about his death amongst the people around, too, Lateen realized, anger was nibbling at him. He'd thought the reputation of Glen Lateen, the mankiller, was consigned to the past. But he was in Texas. And it hadn't been.

He set his chin. "You'll mebbe learn," he said evenly, "if our acquaintance lasts, Blackstock, that I'm a survivor and that I don't kill easy."

With that he turned his gaze back to the lawman. He felt suddenly weary. He had a strong urge to be out of here. He wanted to see Helen and Ma — if she was still alive — and maybe learn from them what was going wrong on this range. Then again — and his uncharacteristic indecision annoyed him — he had this niggle at the back of his mind, too, that he really didn't want to know, and definitely didn't want to get involved in the problems here. Mary and John Gullet were waiting for him back in Radiant Valley, Wyoming, and that was good enough for him. He decided once he'd seen Ma, or visited her grave if she was dead, there would be nothing else to hold him here, and this would be the last time he would visit the East Mora Valley. He had seriously begun to wonder about the wisdom of the decision he had made to travel to here now. Texas was a place where the memory of things took a long time to die. Some memories never did.

"Marshal Tucker," he said, "before I leave for the Double L, there's something else I bound myself to tell you. There's a small sheep farm nestled in the narrow valley Fisher Creek runs through. I found a man by the name of Jim Wayne dead there, hangin' from a cottonwood. The place was burned down. I promised Miz Wayne I'd let you know her plight."

Barret Tucker's eyes narrowed, his jaw lengthened. "My God," he said.

5

IT was plain to Lateen — by the marshal's reaction — the man in the street hadn't seen him and informed him of the Wayne family's plight. Clearly shaken Barret Tucker turned and stared at Blackstock. He breathed, "Do you know anything about this?"

Blackstock's bluff face reddened. "Now hold on, Tucker," he protested. "What the hell would I know about it? You can't go around asking questions like that."

Barret Tucker blinked thick lids over grey eyes. "Why not?" he challenged. "The Double L ain't known for their sweetness an' light. It's common knowledge you've been doggin' the Waynes for months."

Horst Blackstock glared. "Damn it, we want their land and their water,

61

sure," he said. "We've made no secret of that — but we ain't into hangin' them for it."

Marshal Tucker hefted the long shotgun in his hand, clearly unimpressed. "Well, I've only your say-so on that," he growled. "Facts are, as I see them, the Double L have made it plain recently the Waynes, and everybody else on this range, are considered squatters, or rustlers — even the Q Lazy R — though God only knows how you've come to that conclusion."

At that Horst Blackstock became clearly angry. His reddened face set into vicious lines. "I believe a lot of the squatters here are stealin' Double L beef. But we fall short of lynchin' them for it."

Tucker scowled. "So why are you fillin' your bunkhouse with all the border scum you can find?"

Blackstock glared fiercely. "We need those guns," he snorted. "Let's get one thing straight, Tucker — your law extends to the town's boundaries.

What happens in the valley, we take care of."

"Mebbe one time, Blackstock," Tucker said. A grim smile of triumph came to the lawman's broad face. "But you're talkin' to a U.S. marshal now. I got my appointment through from Fort Worth this mornin' an' they want me to see into the mess that's startin' to foul up the valley."

Blackstock stared for a moment. Lateen saw the dark menace at the back of that stare before the large man managed to hide it. Blackstock beamed a big smile before pushing out a beefy hand.

"Well, let me be the first to congratulate you, Barret," he said. "Maybe we'll get some real action on this rustlin' now. You'll find the Double L has nothin' to hide an' willin' to cooperate."

Tucker made a disparaging noise in his throat. As if he had finished with Blackstock for the moment he turned. Lateen met the marshal's gaze as it swivelled on to him. "An' the great Glen Lateen," he said. He didn't try to hide his contempt. "You come back to join the fold? Another damned gunhand for the Double L?"

The blunt remarks sent angry resentment coursing through Lateen. But he roped his temper down. After years of letting his temper rip, he'd learnt, with the help of John Gullet, to do that. At one time he wouldn't have, and that had always been the trouble.

"Tucker," he said evenly. "You've got no call to spur-rake me like that. When my business here is done, I'll be gone. Mora Valley — and the troubles in it — is no concern of mine an' hasn't been for fifteen years."

Tucker's thick lips under the big moustache curled into a sneer. "You want me to believe that?" he growled. "A son, and known mankiller to boot? How long have you been in the valley, Lateen? Concernin' the Wayne family, maybe you're already under orders."

Glen tightened thin lips. "By God,

64

Tucker," he warned, "you'd better draw in those horns. I ain't into lynchin'."

At that Lateen drained the beer mug in his left hand and prepared to leave. But the lawman stepped in front of him and persisted pugnaciously, "With your reputation and your appearance here, there's only one conclusion I can arrive at." He pointed at Palau's bloody body. "Damn it, you've already killed one man, though I ain't grievin' over that — it's just one less scum to deal with. But step out of line any further in this valley an' — "

"Don't threaten me, Tucker," Lateen said quietly, but with steely menace. "I ain't the man to look for on this midden."

After a long, cold stare around the faces circling him Lateen holstered his Colt and strode to the door. At it he turned. "I'll bid you a good day."

Blackstock's harsh demand checked him: "You ridin' out to the Double L?"

"You figure I should be goin' elsewhere?"

Blackstock's stare was bleak; certainly not filled with the milk of human kindness. "No need for that," he said. "Just tell them I'll be delayed, and why."

Lateen scowled. He said, "Deliver your own messages, Blackstock."

He gazed lengthily at the husband of his sister. Something was still prodding his memory about him. It was Blackstock's bluff face — older now but definitely known to him. But where . . . and for why eluded him.

Slightly exasperated by his faulty memory Lateen went through the batwing doors into the burning south Texas mid-afternoon sunlight, feeling grimly stirred up and resentful. With people like Blackstock and Palau at the Double L — and relations to boot — the mire had got thick here in Mora Valley.

He set his grim features. Helen and Ma must have gone crazy, taking such scum on board. And his brother, Abel, he fumed as he prepared to mount his roan, what was he thinking of? And, what if the Double L *had* sanctioned the lynching at the Wayne place . . . ?

Somehow Lateen found he couldn't bring himself to believe it. But feeling short-fused by it all, Lateen stared around him. Already he sensed the town's citizens knew who he was and, he realized, nothing had changed in five years. In Texas he was still a mankiller, a mean man with a gun.

The man, for some, to seek out and kill.

The whole range had an odd feeling of doom about it. He had felt his backbone prickling the moment he had ridden out of the foothills and into the valley before he had even come across the Wayne place.

Yes, there was a taut nervousness all around that seemed to permeate the very air here. In some damned odd way it was as though the whole area had been waiting for somebody like him to come along — some gun-sharp avenger with Judge Colt's gavel ready to beat out a deadly verdict on the evil he sensed was in the Mora Valley.

It was the damndest, craziest feeling. A chill fear penetrated him. He attempted to shrug the feeling off. He had come to Mora Valley to spend time with his dying mother, or to say a prayer over her grave if she was dead, that was all. As soon as he had done that he would be gone — back to Radiant Valley, to his beloved Mary and John Gullet.

Twelve years ago he had left this place behind and vowed never to return. It had only been his fond regard for Helen, and the inescapable fact that he was flesh from his mother's womb — and because of that owed her for the life she had given him — that had brought him back.

Grim-faced he swung up atop the roan. Tall in the saddle he headed down the street looking neither right nor left, leading the pack mule. But as he rode past the buildings he could not help but feel uneasy eyes were following his progress. And it enhanced those previous feelings he'd had. It seemed, if he wasn't careful here, he was going to be sucked into something he didn't want.

He rode out into the big valley with a growing uneasiness. He stared moodily at the range reaching out each side of the trail, to form long blue folds, heaving towards the hills and mountains. Only the scent of the sagebrush pleasured him. But the feeling his gun was going to be wanted here rode with him, whether he liked it or not.

He stared around him angrily. Damn it, his death-dealing, gun-toting days were over. Long gone. Left behind. Range wars were bloody, squalid affairs. And if that was what was going on here — and it seemed likely it was, or would be — he didn't want to be implicated, even though the Double L, it seemed, clearly was.

And further dismaying him, for the Double L to be in dispute with the

Q Lazy R, the Francome place, the family with whom they had been friends for years, settling in the big Mora Valley along with them in the early years . . . well, that took some hard swallowing.

And Lateen found no comfort in his thoughts as he cantered the roan towards the westering sun sinking down towards the mountains seventy miles in the distance to his left.

6

LATEEN was topping the ridge that split the valley — the presence of which had so far hidden the Double L buildings on the East Mora from his view — when the rifle barked, rapping echoes through the black, jagged rocks. Lead spurted earth up from the trail before him.

His now gaunt, tired roan — exchanged for his worn-out chestnut mare at the New Mexico border by a friendly rancher — shied, squealed and reared. Lateen held his seat in the saddle with difficulty. He found it needed an iron hand to calm her. The mule was just pulling and waggling its ears.

From the rocks some twenty yards to Lateen's left the voice ordered, "Far enough, mister. I'm coverin' you purty good."

Cold anger jarred through Lateen's

body. Again a gun was on him. This valley seemed damned!

"What now?" he said bleakly.

The voice snapped, "Your business here?"

With tired effort, Lateen rapped, "Visitin', damn it!"

The voice rose a pitch, became filled with menace. "Don't git sharp with me, hombre. You'll have to do better than that to be believed."

"You think I've a need to?" Lateen threaded the irritation and tired scorn he felt into his reply.

Abruptly the lookout displayed himself by coming out from behind a big boulder at the side of the trail. Lateen saw that his Volcanic rifle was levelled directly at his midriff and that it would be used without compunction if need be.

"You think you're a clever bastard, huh?" the man rasped. "Mebbe you'll find *this* enlightenin'."

The rifle cracked again and Lateen felt his low-crowned black stetson leave his head.

Startled by the sudden, vicious aggression the meeting had taken on, and the heat of the bullet passing quarter-inch close to his skull, Lateen's gaze hardened up to ice-grey. His jaw lengthened. Death dwelt in his cold look. Again he had difficulty holding his nervous horse and the burdened mule.

"By God, man," he breathed, straining hard to control his growing anger, "you're not makin' any friends here."

The lookout grinned. "I ain't paid to." He waggled the gun. "Climb down, smart ass," he grated. He jacked another cartridge into the breech. "Yuh kin walk the rest of the way to the Double L."

Lateen blinked, but remained astride. Instead of moving he said, "You know somethin'? That was a *ten* dollar hat you just blowed off my head. I ought to whip your ass for that."

Still seemingly unaware of the creeping deadliness that had come to Lateen the lookout leaned back. A wide grin spread across his fat face — a face grizzled with dark stubble blueing a greasy double chin.

"A *ten dollar* hat?" he said. His mocking scorn was thick. "Well, damn me! Am I sorry about thet. Hawww . . . hawww . . . hawww!" After moments his raucous laughter faded to nothing and his eyes narrowed. "Well, lissen good fella, you should jest feel lucky it weren't yuh haid . . . !"

Again he seemed inclined to guffaw.

Lateen found now the usual level, icy calmness of old had settled in him. And his eyes were steel-grey, unblinking. This, he knew, was the split-second chance he had been waiting for since the first shot of warning from the lookout had rang out. And it had come sooner than he had expected, for the watchman's ribald hilarity formed a momentary lack of attention on his part.

And Lateen wasn't laughing, nor lacking attention.

With one movement, as fast as an eye-blink, Lateen's Colt was out, a calloused thumb cocking the hammer in the same movement, and his lead was ripping through the lookout's lower right arm, splashing blood and tearing cloth and exposing shattered yellow bone there.

Instantly, the watchman screamed his pain. He staggered back several paces, dropping the rifle and clasping his bloody arm.

"Not so damned funny now, huh, buddy?" Lateen snarled harshly, loud enough to penetrate the man's cries.

Stark-eyed the lookout was now standing moaning and swaying by the side of the trail, his fat, bewhiskered face twisted with pain and anguish, clearly stunned and shocked.

"Oh, God," he groaned. "Yuh've broke it." But dragging up whatever spirit he had left in him he glowered up, fierce hate changing the look in his eyes. "Damn you to hell for that, mister."

Ignoring the ringing curse Lateen rapped, "Shed your sidearm. Smart!"

The lookout moaning loudly now unshipped his Colt with difficulty, having to use his good left hand.

"Throw it," demanded Lateen.

Grudgingly the man did as he was bid, then he gasped, "Who the hell are you, mister? I want to know."

"You should have asked that straight off," advised Lateen. "Maybe it would have saved you a lot of grief. Now pick up my hat, hand it up and get your horse before I break your other arm."

To encourage him Lateen spurted dust with two shots placed between the man's legs — the ground they hit already spattered with the lookout's blood.

Gasping his pain but dancing with alacrity, accompanied by a yelp, the sentry stooped and picked up the hat. He handed it over. Now — crouched against his pain — he made towards the rocks behind him holding his shattered, bloody arm. Lateen followed him close, nudging the roan gently forwards with his knees. The pack mule followed.

Behind the boulders Lateen saw the man's stocky piebald tethered to mesquite.

While moaning "Oh, God, Jesus", over and over, the man attempted to mount. But with a sharp, agonised cry he twisted against the horse's side, after losing his footing in the box stirrup.

White with the pain now and whimpering the lookout made a further effort until, settled in his saddle, he met Lateen's iron-hard gaze with a sullen, defiant stare.

"Now what?" he said.

Lateen waved the Colt. "Head out."

"Where?"

"The Double L."

Lateen saw a kind of hope shine in the lookout's eyes for a moment. "Yuh'll be shot to hell if you go down there," he crowed before pain gasped him to silence again.

A faint smile ghosted Lateen's hard face. "You figure?" he quizzed. "Let's test it."

Now unsure, because of Lateen's

brisk, confident reaction, the man whined, "What about my hardware? I paid plenty for those guns."

"You can pick 'em up later — if you've a mind to. Now move."

Over the ridge Lateen saw the Double L in the distance, maybe a mile away. As he got nearer he gasped his surprise at its size, though he admitted to himself immediately afterwards there was no real reason for him to do so. For money from years of branding and trail-driving mavericks and later enhancing their stock through the introduction of the Hereford breed — and pushing them, too, up the cattle trails to Kansas and to army forts — the Double L must inevitably have prospered from their labours after the war. And it was clear they had done.

It was just that it had been a single-storeyed rundown shack the last time he had seen it. And the large barns and outbuildings he saw were further expressions of the affluence now enjoyed down there.

He could see a long, low bunkhouse down near the river, too. And a quarter of a mile away two wind pumps squealed in the lazy wind, supplying long troughs filled with water that sparkled in the sun. Pipes to irrigation ditches ran half a mile towards fenced hay meadows. Around the troughs the earth was churned, wet mud. At the moment, maybe seventy horses were standing at their galvanised sides drinking. And out on the big range, going into hazy distance, large herds of cattle daubed brown blotches as they cropped grass, quite a few with white faces.

Also, he could see four riders coming hell-for-leather out through the open, high arched gate from the ranchhouse — which was surrounded by a low adobe wall — and heading straight for them, no doubt galvanised by the shooting.

When they arrived to surround him, Lateen said, his eyes steely, "You got a choice, gents. Leave me be — " he flicked his Colt towards his prisoner " — and friend here lives. If you don't he dies an' I don't give a damn about the rest."

"He means it, boys," bawled the lookout, now near to fainting with pain and loss of blood. "Honest to God, he means it."

Though reluctantly, and after hard-eyed assessment, the reception committee backed off, hands warily away from hardware.

"Move in front," Lateen ordered.

With resentful stares and growls the riders complied. One said, "You figure to get away with this?"

Lateen spat and twisted his tired, beard-stubbled face into a grin. "Well, so far, so good," he said with a warm affability that didn't match his icy stare.

As Lateen drew nearer to the ranch he saw three women standing by rocking chairs on the long terrace under the verandah that ran the length of the house. They came to the top of the four steps that gave the house access to ground level from the sloping ground it was built against.

Two more riders broke away from the horses at the trough some two hundred yards away and came up the slope towards them. As they came close they looked hard at the sagging, wounded lookout, then at the other riders, then into Lateen's cold eyes.

"You got some explainin' to do, mister," one said, nudging his horse closer. He was a young, tall, fresh-faced man with narrow, startling blue eyes. The tied-down holster and Smith & Wesson at his hip shouted shootist.

Lateen compressed thin lips before he spoke. "Hands off hardware, boys," he growled. "Heed me."

The spokesman, unlike the four riders Lateen had first encountered, and who were clearly punchers, grinned at him mirthlessly. He said, looking round, "Hell, we got a 'gator by the tail here, boys."

Lateen waved his Colt meaningly.

"Get in front. No tricks."

The gunsel still grinned lazily. "Do as the pilgrim says, boys. We got a real mean one here."

On the worn ground before the house, Lateen drew rein. The riders came to a halt before him and lined up. Lateen watched them turn to face him. Some rested hands on saddle horns, other hands hovered near hardware.

Lateen noticed the shootist's stare had never left him. Now the man said, over his shoulder, "What do you want us to do with him, Miz Lateen?"

On the terrace Lateen recognised Helen — still a tall, strikingly handsome woman — and his Ma right off. The other woman he saw was a stranger. Small, slim, dark haired with luminous black eyes that were looking at him penetratingly. His ma, he saw immediately, was a lot paler and thinner than he remembered. She looked ill. But she was still alive. Somehow, he hadn't expected that.

The first reaction came from Helen.

When she recognised him her high cheek-boned, attractive face broke into a relieved smile. "Glen!" she cried. "You came!"

She came bounding down the steps towards him. Then she stopped and stared, shocked, to see the lookout's hand-squeezed wound and ashen face. It was as though she was seeing it for the first time.

"Jeff," she said. "What happened?"

Lateen interjected, harshly, "He shot my hat off. A damn-fool thing to do."

Helen gasped, swung round, disbelief on her face. She stared at him with the piercing grey-blue eyes of a Lateen. "You wounded him for that?" she said. "Oh, Glen, I thought maybe you'd have . . . changed."

Lateen realized immediately what he had said hadn't sounded good, putting it as he had, but that was the way it was, and — in his book — should have been. But he was sorry to see the shooting had upset Helen. But it didn't alter his attitude.

"When a man starts to fire guns at another man," he said evenly, "he should realize it's the least he can expect in return. The fact is he's lucky to be alive."

Helen's face melted into a look of despair. "Oh, Glen," she said, subdued. "After all these years . . ."

Lateen watched his mother step down off the terrace. Her face was long and white and severe. When she spoke, Lateen found her voice was still as hard and sour and brittle as ever.

"You got gall to turn up here," she breathed. Then she pointed at the shot up arm of the lookout. "And when you do, all you can do is shoot one of my hands." Her cold stare widened. "Well, go back to your Devil, for you are still not welcome here."

With a cry Helen swung round on her. "Mother!" she pleaded. "Jeff shouldn't have shot at Glen. He was wrong doing that."

Lateen watched his mother turn, her eyes pale and wide and questioning, to

Helen. "You sent for him?"

Helen nodded. "Yes."

Lateen saw his mother's thin lips whiten to a thin slit. "You knew he was not welcome here," she said.

Lateen was surprised to see Helen was not cowed by the threat from his mother. One time she would have been. His sister dropped her arms to the side of her blue satin dress and glared, her anger clear. "This is Glen, your son!" she shrilled. "All the way from Wyoming to see you! Is this the way to greet him?"

The words appeared to have no effect. Lateen stared into the pale, severe face of his mother as she turned to him again, ignoring Helen's stark plea. She had the direct, grey-blue eyes he and Helen had inherited. Her hands were clasped like eagle talons around a small bible, held on her lap. Her dress was still black and puritan, but her swept-back hair pulled into a bun at the back was pure white, not the bright, raven dark it had been.

"She tell you I was dyin'? Come to pick over my bones?" she said.

Lateen felt his gut tighten. A sad despair, laced with resentment, coursed through him. She hadn't changed one bit.

"I came to pay my respects to the woman who bore me," he said. "Further than that I want nothing from the Double L."

A sneer creased his mother's thin, pale face. "You came to see what's here for you," she sneered. "Are you still trying to lie your way through life?"

Before Lateen could answer, his mother turned away from him and stared at Helen, though he knew she was still speaking to him. "Well, though I am dyin'," she said over her small shoulder, "I ain't going to do it yet."

Lateen felt a cold anger begin to deepen in the pit of his stomach. But he found he had to admit one grudging thing: the old woman was rawhide right through. However, he decided, he should have stayed in

Wyoming. John Gullet and Mary had warmth and love he knew he would never find here. But he was curious.

"OK, Ma," he said. "You still seem to think you've got me labelled good. But tell me one thing: why do the God-fearing and pure that dwell here need to have armed and dangerous men guarding the trail? You ain't turned hypocrite, have you? I thought guns an' killin' were supposed to be only my trade — and the Devil's, of course. Has he been taken up in service to the Lord?"

At his cutting sarcasm Lateen saw anger flash into those cold grey-blue eyes staring up at him. "You blasphemous . . . It's to protect what's mine!" his mother barked. "I've the right." She raised the small bible. "It's all here."

Lateen narrowed eyelids. He continued caustically, "Well, I only have your word on that, not bein' a student. But why has it come to guns? I'm damned curious."

His mother stared. "Wash your mouth out!" she blazed. "Don't use your profanity here."

At that Helen moved forward to him. Lateen felt her clasp his worn, dusty boot, clamped in the stirrup. "It's crazy, Glen," she shouted. "The whole valley's gone crazy. Horst — "

"What about Blackstock?" Lateen snapped, his curiosity about her husband rising still further.

Not letting Helen reply his mother barked, "He's a God-fearing man! A fine man, who has served us well since he came amongst us and is continuing to do so. Not long after Horst came here he found our neighbours out for what they are, and what I was beginning to suspect — that they were just cattle thieves and squatters."

Feeling bitter Lateen barked, "Like the Wayne family in the foothills, by Fisher Creek?"

Helen, hearing the name and the ringing accusation in Lateen's voice, looked startled before a kind of worried curiosity filled her oval, pretty face.

"What — what about the Waynes, Glen?" she said. Her enquiry was nervous, tentative, as though she had been waiting to hear something like it but didn't want to hear it.

Lateen felt a slight softening towards Helen but kept his stare on his mother. "I found Jim Wayne hanging from a cottonwood," he said, his voice relaying the deep anger in him. "The place burnt out. The widow, the boy Abe, and the little button shocked to hell an' waitin' for Barret Tucker to go out to them."

Helen made a tortured, animal noise in her throat. "Oh, God, no!"

Lateen watched his mother's face alter, become angry.

"You think we had something to do with a thing like that?" she demanded, her voice shrill. "Is that all you think of us? We have always feared God and stood by his word. I find that accusation, coming from a known mankiller contemptible. I . . . "

His mother paused as though lost for words, her face white. He could see she was trembling, her small hands clenched. Then she said, "May the Lord have mercy on you."

Lateen ignored the condemnation.

"Have mercy on *me*, Ma?" His quiet, mirthless laughter was derisive. "I find that mighty rich. You mentioned squatters and cattle thieves. Is that what the Waynes are in your book? Well, I was told the men that did the lynching came with Double L hides over their saddles, claiming they had been found on Jim Wayne's land and that he had butchered them."

His mother lifted a defiant, pale face. "We *have* found hides up there," she said. "Horst has found them. And Fisher Creek has always been Double L range. But there has been no order from this ranch to do that to Jim Wayne. That business on Fisher Creek is in the hands of Clark Fulton, the county sheriff."

"What I heard, county law don't

mean much," growled Lateen.

His mother's stare was level and steady. "You blaming me for that?"

Lateen glared. "Then who *has* hung Jim Wayne?" His voice now rang with the anger he felt. "And ain't this East Mora range you're on enough for you? I can't recall Pa ever laying any claim to the northern foothills."

And that sent his memory back. He had always understood his Pa and Henry Francome of the Q Lazy R had agreed to split the Mora Valley into east and west, the hog back down the middle the divide for the two ranges. The hills around had always been free range as far as they were concerned.

His mother's face narrowed. "The fact of the matter is our stock needs the water," she said. "The water we have is hardly enough."

Contempt filled Lateen. "There was always plenty of water on this range," contradicted Lateen. "More'n enough."

His mother nodded. "Was is right," she said. "But there was an earth tremor in the mountains summer before last. The ground just opened up and Whitewater River dived straight into the fissure and has continued to do so ever since. And as you know the Whitewater always was our lifeline when the creeks dried up. As a consequence, the north range now has no water at all, only Fisher Creek."

His mother's face was now drawn, her eyes narrow. "We've offered the Waynes more than a fair price for their land and water but the fools won't sell. All they seem intent on doin' is taking our beef while they graze what bit of good land there is with their sheep."

Lateen blinked lids over his cold gaze. No remorse in his Ma, no nothing about Jim Wayne's lynching. Just talking land, water, and ultimately, no doubt, the money it made.

"Did you hear me, Ma?" he breathed intensely. "Jim Wayne is dead, the rest of his family homeless. They've told me it was Double L riders that came and did it."

As he spoke Lateen felt Helen's grip tighten on his boot. He looked down. Her grey-blue stare looked shocked as it reached up to his.

"That's a terrible thing to suggest, Glen," she gasped. "What you suspect has got to be wrong. Horst, or any of us, wouldn't order anyone killed. We deal strictly legitimately."

But Lateen found he was only made curious by his sister's response. "Blackstock again?" he said. "What say has he in the business affairs of the Double L?"

"As my husband, and as ranch manager, a lot," Helen said. "He is a member of the family. Naturally he is brought in on all the decisions regarding the ranch."

His mother's voice snapped irritably, bringing Lateen's stare round to her. "As I have said Horst Blackstock is a fine, God-fearing man and has my full approval. And if you want to know the reason, it's simple. I was finding, with the years pilin' on me, that it was becoming hard to cope with the rapid growth of the Double L's affairs. I had to bring in a manager. Well — and in this I thank the Lord — Horst turned out to be just the man and, to God's further glory, fell in love with Helen and she returned that love and I was happy to give my blessing. Now I rely heavily on his business acumen. And seeing you again and finding your ways have not changed, I — "

Lateen blinked. "You what, Ma?"

She turned away, as if sickened. "Nothing," she said, her voice hollow.

Lateen stared at her, but it was clear she had no more to say. But his gut feeling about Blackstock and this memory of something bad about him pushing at the back of his mind, something about the man once being head high in villainy rankled.

"And Abel?" he said. "Where does he fit in? Shouldn't *he* be headin' the brand?"

His mother's chin came up defiantly, but there was something akin to deep hurt clouding her gaze before she masked it with her iron will.

"Your brother, Abel," she said, "is a drunkard and has gone to the Devil, like his father and his brother. He is now totally incapable of attending to the affairs of the Double L."

The news shook Lateen. He watched his mother's chin lift even higher. "As you will appreciate by looking around, the Double L is no longer the two-bit concern it was and needs steady hands."

With that his mother paused. Lateen met her hard stare as it reached up and found his own gaze. For a moment he thought he detected some sad regret for the lost, barren years between them before the emotion was brought under that steely control of hers and hidden again.

Then she said, her tone subdued, "The one child I thought could have made something of himself and the Double L, turned instead to mankilling." She paused and lowered her gaze, her bottom lip trembling for a moment before she added, "Well, that son is now long dead to me and has no place on this range while I'm alive."

With that, she turned her back on him.

Lateen felt the hollow emptiness he had endured twelve years ago when he had first heard that ultimatum. Now, clearly, with the years, the bitter cancer it had started between them then when he had turned and left them instead of staying on and taking their censure no matter what, had eaten deeply.

He tightened his lips, stuck out his hard jaw. Though there had been that brief flash of tenderness in his mother's eyes moments ago it had gone as quick as it had come. And now, he found, to be spoken of as an abstract, dead object was slightly sickening.

There had been a time, he recalled, his heart tugging, when as a small boy, there had been a deep well of love to be tapped in her. But with the early death of his father and the responsibility of having a young family and the harsh fight to live on a Texas range thrust upon her, the experience had calloused her. And as those early years had ground her down, she had turned to God for solace and strength.

And she had gradually become this puritanical, bitter woman he saw before him. Maybe he, too, being the wild boy he was, had also helped to scar her. With the hindsight of maturity he now realized his own conduct in those days had not been exemplary. His hell-raising must have been horrendous to her religious sensitivities, and her pride, and added to the deep burden she was already carrying. And he had been little help around the ranch as well, because of his go-to-hell ways. But if, when he had returned from the war with that hell subdued a little, and she had been willing to show some of the Lord's forgiveness, things might have worked out differently.

With a sigh he leaned down and kissed Helen on the forehead, then squeezed her shoulders. "I tried, sister," he said. "I'm sorry."

Helen nodded numbly and dropped her hand from his boot.

Then he lifted his gaze to his mother. "I need a change of horse," he said. "I pushed the roan hard to get here."

His mother's nod was grudging. "Take your pick of the remuda." Then she flicked a glance at the wounded lookout, now quietly moaning and almost lying flat along his horse's back with the faintness he was fighting. "Somebody patch up Wells and take him into Craddock," she ordered. "Get Doc Rutherford to fix him up."

Lateen met her gaze as it returned to him. He couldn't help it. He nodded towards the tall, young, pale-eyed shootist who was still leaning forward, gazing intently at him. He found he couldn't prevent the words coming out.

"That one," he said. "He's a man-killer. I know the look. Why does he fit in here an' not me?"

His mother's face lengthened, but looked slightly startled before the mask closed down again on her thin face. She said briskly, "Horst deals with the choosing of the hands."

Lateen smiled but the smile was cynical and mirthless. "Maybe he needs somebody around to point out the difference between cowpokes and killers," Lateen said. "That man there could string Wayne up, no regrets. Maybe has."

The gunslinger reared up in the saddle, leaned forward. "Mighty big words, *hombre*," he said. "Hope you can back 'em up, some day."

Lateen turned cold, challenging eyes towards the shootist, but the drum of approaching hooves turned all heads. Lateen switched his gaze to see Horst Blackstock running his horse down the long slope off the ridge. Soon he was pulling the big mare to a halt before them.

Breathing hard the big, bluff man climbed down. First he stared at Luke, the shot lookout being helped across the yard, then turned querying eyes to Lateen's mother.

"What happened?"

Lateen found his mother's stare upon him. "My son," she said, "has been practising his trade once more.

7

AT the news Horst Blackstock's bluff face seemed to swell, grow more red. He swung his cold gaze on to Lateen's mother. "Ma'am, I don't care if he is your son, and it maybe hurts you for me to say it," he said angrily. "But I say damn him. Did he tell you about August?"

Lateen watched his mother's blue-grey stare turn to hold Blackstock's dark gaze. She frowned. "What about Mr Palau?"

Blackstock said, "Your boy just shot and killed him in Craddock."

A scream came from the dark-haired girl standing in the shadows of the long terrace. Hearing it, Lateen watched Helen turn abruptly and run up the steps to her. She took the woman in her arms and held her. Blackstock followed Helen and put a comforting arm on his

101

niece's shoulder.

Then Lateen became aware that his mother's stare was once again upon him. She said, her anger and pain clear in her eyes, "Roast you for the Devil's agent you are! Get off this range!"

Lateen feeling as though his emotions had once more been shredded bare, gazed bleakly into his mother's blazing eyes. "He wouldn't be put off," he said harshly. "In the end, it was him or me."

"Even so, you had to kill him, didn't you, like the murdering killer you are!" His mother's demand was strident.

Lateen's voice grated. "Yes!"

His mother's pale face lengthened. The look in her eyes grew as cold and grey as ice on a frozen river.

"In the name of God," she breathed, her voice quiet and quaking. "Go! You give me nothing but misery."

Lateen nodded slowly. She would never see his side. And because of that he felt the emptiness again inside him, barren as a stony desert. But with a sort of sad, perverse pleasure he found there was one thing he could add to this. "I wonder what you will do or say, Ma, if the killin' of Jim Wayne is laid at the door of the Double L?" he said.

His mother's eyes glared for a moment but her features remained the mask it had settled into at the news of Palau's shooting. "It won't be," she said. With that she turned to the men who now circled him. "See this killer off my land," she ordered curtly.

Lateen heard gunmetal click all around him. At the sound he felt the cold fingers of fear crawl up his backbone.

"You give the orders, Miz Lateen," the shootist said. "*Clear* off the range, ma'am?"

"Clear off the range, Spencer," she said to the gunslinger.

Lateen's ears pricked up at the name. *L. T.* Spencer? He'd heard of him. One of the newer breed of gunslingers. They didn't come any deadlier, so he'd heard from men who knew. And it was a name a man tended to remember because of Spencer's insistence on the use of his initials only. The knowledge left him grim and bitter.

He watched the circle of hard-eyed riders close in. One reached over and relieved him of his guns, while the others began nudging at Lateen's tired roan and pack mule with their horses.

Holding his ground Lateen stared at his mother. "I asked for a change of horse," he said.

Without answering, his mother glared once before turning her back on him. She walked towards the terrace where Helen held Blackstock's weeping niece in her arms. And Blackstock was by her side, too, his hand now gently on her heaving shoulders, his face a picture of concern and sympathy. The woman's heavy sobs rang across the bare ground to Lateen. But they barely touched him.

"I hope you know what you're doin', Ma," he called. "I truly do."

With that he lifted his gaze to look

at the back of his sister. "For what it's worth, Helen," he shouted so she could hear, "Palau gave me no choice. You gotta believe that."

There was no response from Helen, only the crouching of her fine shoulders, as though his words were physically pummelling her.

Seeing he was not going to get an answer, Lateen turned his gaze on to Blackstock, ignoring the horses and riders now pushing harder at him. "I know you from somewhere, mister, an' it ain't good," he said. "When I remember, I'll be back."

Lateen saw the words bought a faint flicker of what could be construed as puzzlement, even fear into Blackstock's eyes before his lips twisted into a sneer. He was clearly not intimidated by the threat.

"Get that damned killer off this land, boys," he growled. He swung his gaze on to L. T. Spencer. "Give him a Blackstock reminder not to come back."

Lateen noticed the effect on the gunsel was like that of a cat that had been given cream. "Yo, Horst," he said. L. T. Spencer grinned. "That way, mister." He pointed with his Smith & Wesson towards the north.

Though he felt the cold grip of fear in the pit of his stomach — for there was something sinister in Blackstock's last words — Lateen allowed a grim smile to stretch his thin lips, but only to hide his unease. "Hell," he said. "I just come from there."

L. T. Spencer matched his grin, as though he wanted to play along with his grim humour. "In that case," he crowed, "you'll know the way. Just head out there, mister."

After a long, deathly stare at the gunsel Lateen nudged his knees into the weary roan's flanks. When he did the hardcases circling him fell back and closed in behind him.

It was as they passed one of the huge barns that Lateen saw his brother Abel limp out of the door. Lateen could see he wore a wooden peg to replace his shot-off left foot. And the sad sight of him caused Lateen to narrow his eyes even more than they naturally were. For Abel looked terrible. He had the bloated, purpling face of a long-time drinker. He looked nearer fifty than thirty three. And he seemed to take long moments before he recognised him. When he did, he frowned at the escort before turning his gaze back to him.

"Glen?" he said. "What's goin' on? Why the guns?" Then he stepped forward, hand pushed out, a smile on his face. "But, damn it, man, it's good to see you."

He began to push his way through the riders, his hand extended. Lateen watched L. T. Spencer bar his way with the big buckskin gelding he was riding, before his brother could reach him.

"Give him space," rasped Lateen.

A gun barrel stabbed at his back. "Shet it, wide-mouth."

The flesh crawled where the gun prodded. Lateen watched the smile still creasing L. T. Spencer's face widen. It had a certain inaneness. And it didn't express mirth. At the moment all it expressed was contempt. For Abel?

"Now hold on, Mr Lateen," L. T. Spencer said affably. "Your Ma has just given clear strict instructions to hustle your brother here clean off this spread. An' she said nothin' about stoppin' on the way."

Abel glared up at the gunman, but Lateen thought he saw a slight hint of fear, too, in his brother's eyes. "Damn it, Spencer," Abel protested, "that's my brother."

The shootist nodded. "I know that. But the thing is this brother of yourn has dun shot an' killed poor old August Palau an' your Ma has taken more than a little exception to it. 'Nough to bar him from the Double L for life, I guess."

Lateen met Abel's stare as it switched

to him. "That right, Glen? Did you kill Palau?"

Lateen nodded.

Abel blinked his booze-ravaged, red-rimmed eyes. "Well, good riddance, is all I can feel for him," he said. "One less varmint, I reckon." He glared defiantly at L. T. Spencer now. "If you ask me, there's more around here that need the same treatment."

A soft chuffing laugh came from the shootist. "Wooowee, Mr Lateen. Now you is talkin' about a friend o' mine." The smile faded, the voice went low. "Now you jest go back to your bottle, you damned cripple, an' keep that mouth shut. I wouldn't want to mess up thet ugly face o' yourn."

A flame of anger ignited inside Lateen, but he doused it. There would be a time. If nothing else, he had learned patience during his years at John Gullet's Iron Fork. But he felt now he was far from finished here on the Mora Valley ranges.

He watched as Abel was nudged

unceremoniously aside by the escort. But above the noise of men and creaking saddle leather he shouted, "Banka Wallanka Ballantee, Glen!"

Lateen's ears twitched to hear the silly phrase, though it wasn't silly to him. It was an old code he and his brother had used as children to get away from their parents and to their secret hideout cave on the big ridge that ran down the middle of the valley.

"Two days?" he called. "Afternoon?"

Then he caught L. T. Spencer's narrow, suspicious stare probing him. "What the hell goes on?" he said.

Lateen smiled disarmingly. "Just kid's stuff," he said.

L. T. Spencer's face lost its smile, became sullen. "Kid's stuff, huh?" he growled. "Well, you git, for what you is headed for ain't goin' to be kid's stuff." Then he guffawed in a high-pitched way and stared around the riders with him gleefully. "Right, boys?"

The small, stocky, tough-looking rider next to Lateen, who had poked the gun in his back, nodded. His grin exposed black-grained teeth. "Yeah," he said. "That's right, L.T. It sure ain't goin' to be that. Haaaw, haaaw, haaaw!"

Then he lashed Lateen's roan and mule across their rumps with his quirt and the whole lot of them went galloping up the long valley towards the northern foothills.

But dark unease rode heavily with Lateen.

8

AS Lateen rode — hemmed in by the hardcases — and the miles rolled by, he became more and more uneasy. This wasn't going to be an affable parting; his instinct for the evil that dwelt in some men told him that. And there was evil here, he decided. Almost from the start he had had no doubts about that. There had been something in Blackstock's order, too, to do things *the Blackstock way*, that gave him no comfort. For, in the past, though he could not remember it, there had been something evil he had witnessed Blackstock do.

And as they left the foothills via Conner's Run and arrived at the high, rocky Hell Fire Pass that took the trail over the mountains and out of the valley to the high plains, L. T. Spencer trotted his big horse in front of

Lateen and turned it.

Still smiling, he lined up his fancy Smith & Wesson. Lateen could see, some twenty yards past the shootist and tucked under a long, frowning scarp, was what appeared to be a newly-built line cabin.

At this point, Lateen knew, they were eighteen miles from the ranch.

"Blackstock reckons this is boundary edge," Spencer said.

Lateen narrowed his eyelids. "That so?" he said. "Times change. This was free range, one time."

Spencer's smile faded slightly. Lateen watched his grey, flat stare leave his own. Without seemingly any compunction then L. T. Spencer turned, aimed for the pack mule and shot it through the brain. It collapsed to its knees and keeled over, its legs trembling, its eyes blinking, its mouth slack, the pink tongue lolling on to the grass.

Shocked by the merciless killing Lateen stiffened. "Why, you damned lousy bastard!"

L. T. Spencer brought up the smoking gun. He started grinning again. "Yeah? Anythin' else?"

Lateen knotted his big hands around the reins in them. "By God, someday, man . . . "

L. T. Spencer continued smiling before he sighed. "Sad to say, there ain't goin' to be a someday." The shootist turned. "Pull him off his horse, boys. Let's say farewell the Blackstock way, *then do it mine*."

Lateen saw lariats start snaking out towards him. He gathered the roan to run, but it was useless. He managed to ward off a couple of ropes before he was looped. Then he felt himself being jerked out of the saddle to the ground, which he hit with bone-jarring force.

As he fought to gain his feet he could hear Spencer's high-pitched, excited shout,

"Tow him, boys! Tow him to hell for Palau!"

Even as Spencer shouted Lateen felt the ropes snatching, cutting with fierce

114

pain into his hard, leaned-down body. And he yelled out as, with wild whoops, he saw the rope handlers spur flanks and the ropes tauten even more. With stark fear raging through him Lateen found himself forced to bound along on his long, denim-clad legs, fighting to hold his feet.

But from the first he knew it would be hopeless and he found himself being towed with irresistible force and increasing speed onward, the mountains echoing with his desperate calls and the wild, harsh whooping of the hardcase riders.

Finally the speed of the horses got too much. With a last despairing cry he tripped and sprawled forward, hitting the ground with bone-jarring force before being dragged along.

And seeing him fall only seemed to incense the hardcases even more. They drove spurs viciously into the flanks of their mounts.

Lateen realized now his torso was being pounded unmercifully, and his fear of a horrible death grew large in him.

He began to struggle against the ropes, his desperation growing to panic proportions. He had seen men dragged before, usually hooked up in a stirrup unable to release themselves. And, if it had gone on long enough, what had remained had been a bloody mulch, gut-retching to see.

He hit a rock, another, felt his hat leave his head, felt his body hit more rock — driving the breath out of him, sending burning pain rampaging through him. His shouts for mercy went unheeded.

And all he could do was bawl and rage at his tormentors. Then, abruptly, white light accompanied by jarring pain across his head sent him plunging into dark oblivion.

★ ★ ★

As he came to Lateen realized he was staring at the moon and stars, but their

116

brightness was blurred and indistinct, only just penetrating the narrow slits that were his grossly swollen eyelids. Then he became aware that his arms were pinned to his sides and that his body was throbbing — a mass of raw pain.

And, he realized, he was wrapped in something . . .

Though he was curious — anxious — to know what it was he let his curiosity ride as he waited for his vision to clear, his emotions to come to terms with the towering pain he was suffering. And to orientate himself.

Gradually he began to realize that he was actually lying on his back and that this something he was encased in was something that was wet and greasy and smelling sweetly of blood. And gradually he ascertained he was somewhere in the mountains, and that he was cold and nauseated with pain and . . .

. . . wrapped in this damn thing . . .

To see it, despite the pain, he

struggled to raise his head. Though the agony the attempted movement wrought was weakening in its intensity, he managed to lift his head and stared down at his body. What he saw caused him to go cold with a dreadful fear.

He was wrapped in the green hide of the pack mule. When the mid-summer sun got up tomorrow — despite him being in the mountains — it was going to be powerful enough to dry it and shrink it, and he was going to be squeezed to death in the most appalling way.

Was this the Blackstock way? No, the dragging had been Blackstock's. This was L. T. Spencer's contribution. He was just a black-hearted, out-and-out killer and made no secret of it. He could expect no more from him. It was the snakes you had to watch, not the wolves.

Lateen felt his limbs go weak with fear. Oh, my God, he thought. What was Helen, what was Ma, thinking about — harbouring such a black, murderous pack of bastards? Lateen found it was easy to believe Blackstock could be intensely charming to the ladies, and impressive. He dressed well and he could split his personality down the middle to suit the need of the hour. A charming, suave business man one day, a dark killer the next, ordering executions without conscience if circumstances warranted it.

And where had he seen him before! The name hadn't been Horst Blackstock. It had been an incident during the war. Damn it, if only he could recall.

But, hell, why was he thinking about that?

Waves of nausea struck him. As he waited for the sensations to subside he began to realize that there was a pale, yellow tint starting to colour the eastern sky. Soon it would be daylight. Through the slits that were his eyelids he could still see the sky was star filled, clear — primed for another searingly hot, long day.

More anxiety swept through him. He

had to get out of this skin, despite the pain it caused him as he tested its tightness. And, with a hint of hope growing in him, he realized there was still some give in the green hide, some slight elasticity.

He began to wriggle his body, gasping at the pain his struggles caused. But he knew it was nothing to the pain he would suffer if he didn't shed himself of this perverted torture contraption he was encased in, dreamed up by an incredibly sick mind.

Then, like a bright flame across his pain-dulled brain, it came to him. His gunbelt. He realized it was still around his waist. Maybe if he could unbuckle it and gradually ease it down, it would give him enough room to get out of this thing . . .

The necessity of release that was slowly seeping into him sent a surge of desperate strength through him. He gritted his teeth, to fight against the pain already assaulting him. He began to force his hands — trapped to his sides — up, round towards his navel. Though the animal skin was tight and bonded to him by rawhide stitching, thank God there was enough give and lubrication in the hide yet to assist some movement.

He felt sweat begin to bead his corrugated brow. As it ran off the crinkled flesh it stung the bruised cuts ballooning the flesh around his eyes and face. He ignored it. He was getting his hands to where he wanted them — on the buckle of his gunbelt.

But the sky, all the time, was getting lighter. And all nature was stirring to life. Birds were beginning to sing their songs to greet the new fresh dawn coming with unwanted speed to the eastern sky.

He found, also, despite the mountain cold, his body was becoming bathed in sweat; that it was mingling with his blood and seeping into the cuts and abrasions that covered his torso — adding to the pain he already had. But, with a flicker of elation born out of the discovery, he realized that that sweat, too, was acting as a lubricant.

The sun lipped the peaks before him, sending light flooding across the pine-clothed mountains and into his eyes, causing him to narrow his lids for protection. He must have been unconscious most of the night. That sent him into further straining efforts to escape.

For time, he knew, was running out . . .

Aroused by it, he renewed his efforts, fought the new waves of nausea that surged through him. He steeled up the resolve and stamina he knew he had, and had tested often in his short life. He focused on the goal before him — to get out of this death trap. More than ever now, he thought, as he whimpered and cursed his pain, Glen Lateen had to return to Mora Valley. Now, more than ever, he had unfinished business there. He had scores to settle. Blood must be paid for — with blood. As it also says in his ma's Good Book — maybe not quite the proper words but the right sentiment: *Do as ye are done by*. And, by God, that suited him!

He felt his hands slip up suddenly, slide in front of him. With feverish, fumbling fingers he undid the gunbelt buckle, then, with patient, pain-filled care began to ease the bulky belt down his body as far as he could, gritting his teeth against the pain.

Again nausea hit him as the pain got too much. He relaxed a moment, allowed his bruised, swollen lids to close over his burning eyes. Rest now . . . then one more effort. One more would do it, he felt sure.

He felt something alight on the hide encasing him. He snapped open his eyes immediately. A crow had dropped on to the skin. It had begun picking at it. Horrified fear surged through him. He shouted, rocked his body. With a squawk the feeder on carrion took off, cawing resentfully and settled on top of a rock nearby.

Trembling through exhaustion and

desperation, Lateen began again to work the belt down his body. And all the time he thought the hide was becoming slacker. He tugged with his feet. He had to get them out. Then he realized those who had sewn him in had pulled the hide tight about his ankles, too, as well as round his neck. But, mercy of mercies, if he could slide his feet out of his boots . . .

But there was no way he could do it. It was the stitching, he realized. In reality, all his efforts had been for nothing. The hide still held him like a vice. He had been crazy to think that loosening his gunbelt would solve his dilemma, or attempting to pull up his feet would improve anything. He was stitched in tight, stitched in fast. He had to face it. He was going to die in a most horrible way.

At that thought, and weak as he was from the dragging he had received, he almost sobbed with distress before he injected steel into himself again. There'd be no damned self-pity here.

But he found his anxiety had drained him. He looked with tortured eyes at the crow which was glaring balefully down at him with black, brilliant eyes from the rock. Another joined him, then another until the stunted pines and rocks around began to become thick with them. To add to it, the buzzards began to circle above.

Then it came to him. His claspknife. It was in the watch pocket of his denims. If they hadn't taken it from him, he had a chance.

Moaning, he worked his hands once more, and once more intense pain began to rake his body with fiery fingers, causing him to gasp and quiver with near exhaustion.

He was almost sobbing with the pain when he managed to slide his fingers into the watch pocket of his denims. But the hide was still tight, still pressing against him — wet and slimy . . . and beginning to tighten.

His heart raced and he prayed as he felt for the knife. Thank God, they hadn't taken it. With the tips of his fingers he could feel the rough handle of deerhorn. Almost delirious with relief he wrapped his trembling fingers around it, fighting off the waves of nausea that were trying to drive him into oblivion again. He couldn't let them take him for the sun would burn down on to the hide and that would be it. He would be crushed, slowly, in the most appalling way.

He slid the knife out of his pocket, holding it tenuously between his bruised and cut fingertips. He finally got a better grip on it and tasted the salt of his sweat on his lips as it ran stingingly down his face.

He prised the blade open, nicking his finger. It was razor-sharp, he knew. He kept it that way. But no matter. Now he had to push up, push towards the stitches. He had to cut them. He had to . . . cut . . . the . . . stitches . . .

His head swam. It felt as though it was bursting. He realized, because of his exertions, he was gasping, moaning as he sawed — sobbing even as he fought the restriction of the hide and the vast pain assaulting his body. It would take all the steel will he could muster to keep him going through this one.

Then he felt one stitch give. Whimpering with relief he moved the blade to the next loop. It seemed to take an age to cut. Then he felt another go — felt the vice-like grip of the hide start to ease off him . . .

Two minutes later he lay panting and clear of the tube of death. It was lying flabby and flat beside him on the thin grass carpeting this high place . . .

Now he realized the sky was swimming about in restless waves above him. He couldn't stop it. His body, also, was now a battleground of obscene pain, striving to drive him into oblivion again. And he was surprised to see the sun was already well up off the horizon. Getting out of that skin had taken him longer than he had thought . . .

Curiously he wanted to know; wanted

to know how long it *had* taken him to fight out of that trap of hell. It had suddenly become immensely important to him. While he thought he found himself hovering between oblivion and rationality, and that now he was out of that deathtrap, all his will to survive had relaxed. All he really wanted to do was just rest, sleep. Nothing else seemed to matter . . .

He noticed a buzzard was on the ground nearby, maybe two. It was hopping cautiously towards him its oddly coloured eyes staring at him. He found himself breathing rapidly. He tried to get up. He shouted at it, flapped his arms about.

Then he thought he heard the booming, flat crack of a rifle, thought he heard the screaming and cawing of the crows and buzzards, the rustle of many wings as they scattered. He even felt weight push off his raw, aching body.

He felt revulsion flood through him. Had one of those stinking carrion been on him? God almighty, he couldn't believe it . . .

He began to babble at them, try to fight off the blackness coming in at him from every extremity of his vision.

But he couldn't manage it . . .

9

IT was as though he had been in a dream world. It was as though he had been hovering in a strange, nightmare-ish limbo. There had been soft voices talking, shadowy shapes drifting in and out of this dream world. Often he had been aware of cool cloths dampening the fires on his brow and body, had been aware of broth that had been spooned past his lips before he had slipped away into oblivion again.

But this time the mists clouding his eyes were finally clearing and Lateen realized he was staring at frilly net curtains. They were wafting lazily in the sage-scented, gentle breeze coming in through the open, glazed window at the foot of the bed.

He was between clean, white sheets. Here and there he could feel bandages against his body, too. He realized he was also naked. Gingerly he raised a hand to feel his face. It was still puffed and crusted with scabs.

He tried to lift his head, but cried out as pain fired through him and he lowered it again with a groan. He found his noise brought the young woman in through the door to his right. Though he couldn't see it, he sensed it was there.

Now she was standing by the bed and looking down. He could see she was a petite, well-formed girl in denims and a green, silk blouse, open at the neck. Her face was pretty, framed in dark curls. The eyes, looking at him, were hazel and warm-looking and sympathetic. She was maybe eighteen years of age, he guessed, or a little more. He couldn't tell properly. She had the kind of face that was always hard to judge.

"Where am I?" he croaked.

"The Q Lazy R," she said.

"How long have I been here?"

"Three days."

Shocked by that he made to get up. Pain drove him back. "Three days!" He gasped. He'd made the promise to meet Abel at their secret hideout — that would have been yesterday.

He lay panting from his exertions for a moment then said, "The Q Lazy R? The Francome place?"

"Yes," the girl said. "But be easy. You're still very weak. In fact, Doctor Rutherford said you should be dead."

"Who found me?"

"I did," she said. "I saw the buzzards circling." He watched a frown gather on her brow. "Who did this to you, Glen?"

Glen? She knew him?

But that was of no concern to him at the moment. He compressed his thin lips. "What would it mean to you if I said riders for the Double L?" he said.

The girl gasped and her eyes rounded with disbelief. "The Double L! But, they're kin. Not Helen, not Missus

Lateen . . . they wouldn't . . . " Her voice trailed off. She stood there, still staring, as if not believing her own ears.

"Not them, maybe," he said.

He found strength was slowly returning to him, driven by the bitter hate that was beginning to well up in him when he remembered who had put him here — weak, pounded and pain-ridden.

He studied her open, fresh face. "How d'you know I'm Glen Lateen?"

The girl spread her hands, smiled sunnily, dispelling her concern. "Purty simple," she said. "Pa and my brother Henry told me."

By the second, Lateen found his wits were returning. "You Rosemary?" he said. "Why, you were only knee high last time I saw you."

"That was twelve years ago, Glen Lateen," she reproved him gently. She pushed out the fully mature breasts he could see were swelling under her blouse, as if to prove her womanhood to him. "Eighteen now," she added proudly. Then her face altered again. "But, Glen, how could your family allow this to be done to you?"

Lateen shook his head. Despite his pain and concerns, he found it easy to talk to this girl. "I don't think Ma an' Helen know," he said. Oddly, he found he wanted to tell this slip of a girl the full story now, but that was best said to men. Jud Francome and his son Henry were the people to tell it to and to question in return.

He said, "Is your pa about, Rosemary?"

"He's with the boys up in Wolf Canyon, in the Black Water brakes," she said. "We've lost another sixty head to cow thieves out there recently. He's bringing what there is left nearer to the ranch."

Lateen sighed. "I see," he said. "Accordin' to the Double L, they're the on'y ones bein' hit by rustlers."

The girl nodded, serious-faced. "That's the story Blackstock puts about," she said. "He's even gone as far as to accuse us of doin' it."

Then her features altered, as if it wasn't a woman's worry. She looked eager for gossip. "Heard you shot and killed August Palau." She gestured at his battered, prone body. "That the reason for this?"

"Mebbe," he said. "Just what is goin' on in the valley, Rosemary?"

She looked at him steadily, gnawing her pretty bottom lip. They were lips, Lateen judged, that many a cowboy worth his salt would ride through hell and high water to kiss and maybe some had already tried.

"To tell you plainly, Glen," she said, "and I'm sorry to have to say it, the Double L are causing all sorts of problems in the valley. They've got so land hungry they don't listen to anybody any more."

"You mean Horst Blackstock has," he said harshly.

She nodded again. "Yeah," she agreed. "Pa figures he's behind it all, and has blinded your ma and Helen with his charm. Even so, Pa says he still can't figure it, not with your ma, anyway. Says your ma's always been too careful an' shrewd to be taken in by that sort of stuff. He's sure she would never put her name to what's going on in the valley if she knew. He reckons she just can't know, or chooses to disbelieve anybody who tries to tell her, or is just too ill. And Pa says he'll *never* be able to figure out what Helen saw in Blackstock, never. I can tell you, Glen, Pa has no likin' for that man at all."

"He ain't on his own there," Lateen bit out.

Rosemary faltered a moment, then went on. "Before *he* came," she said " — Blackstock, I mean — Helen was always over here, neighbourin'. And when Ma died seven years ago, she became near to being a mother to me an' helped cook an' clean here while Pa got over the shock of Ma's death. But I hardly ever see her now. She's altered somethin' awful over the last year or so. An' I so loved to go over an' see little James, her boy."

Rosemary stopped and blinked. Lateen could see tears were pearling the edges of her eyelids. They began to trickle down her cheeks. "And, Glen, I'd be a liar if I said I didn't miss it all."

As the information came Lateen cursed silently; cursed what was happening on this range; cursed the hurts throbbing through his body; cursed being helpless here; cursed Horst Blackstock and the trash that rode for him, particularly L. T. Spencer. There'd be some sudden accounting when he ran against that *hombre* again.

"Ma and Helen seem mesmerized by Blackstock," he agreed.

Rosemary sniffed, looking miserable now, and took out a small handkerchief from her denims. "Same words Pa used," she said.

"What about the law here, Rosemary?" he said. "Heard it ain't too good, though I find Barret Tucker a purty even man, though a mite abrasive."

"Sheriff Clark Fulton is over at River Falls, the county seat." She looked up, her eyes questioning. "You maybe don't know not bein' around an' all, but because they brought the railhead into River Falls, they made that the county seat, too — even though it is seventy miles away."

Lateen nodded. Of course, he didn't know. River Falls was new to him, as was the information that Mora Valley was now incorporated into a county, and that the county seat was all those miles away.

"What's this Sheriff Fulton been doin' about things here?" he probed.

Rosemary pouted her pretty young lips. "He sent a deputy over a month ago to investigate the shooting of a Flying S rider — and some rustling on the Squared M, Henry Mellor's place in the foothills way to the south," she supplied. "Pa said that all the deputy did, though, was near drink Craddock dry with the help of Horst Blackstock's money. Pa said that in politics, money and liquor talks — and Blackstock has both and with them is able to influence the votes in this area. Well, the outcome was, the deputy left without making any arrests, or coming to any conclusions, other than it was most likely Mexicans from over the border, and he couldn't touch them. He said Sheriff Fulton would have to deal with the whole affair through the Mexican authorities. The outcome was Henry Mellor said he'd had enough. He sold out to Blackstock, said he was out to try his luck in California an' left."

"Barret Tucker?" ventured Lateen.

He watched her pretty eyes widen, before they clouded with sadness. "Of course, you wouldn't know," she said. "He was found shot and killed by an unknown assailant day before yesterday. He had been out visitin' poor Miz Wayne an' her children on Fisher Creek, an' was returnin' from there."

The news left Lateen cold. From what he had experienced of Barret

139

Tucker, he'd had the marshal tagged as a brave, square player.

"Now that won't be liked," he said.

Rosemary nodded. "He was popular."

Lateen shook his head. "Not because of that," he said. "He had been called upon to be a U.S. marshal."

Rosemary's eyes widened and met his stare. "But I thought he was just a — "

Lateen cut her short. "He got confirmation of his appointment on'y t'other day. Maybe Horst Blackstock has made his first mistake."

Rosemary stared. "Do you think he could have been behind the shooting? Surely he would realize . . . "

"Who else?" Lateen demanded. He found it hard for a slip of a girl not to accept his judgement.

She shook her head. "I don't know. Pa said Barret was beginning to dog Blackstock, going as far as to accuse him, so he heard, of ordering Jim Wayne's lynching. But Blackstock always has an alibi for himself and his crew. Pa said he claimed he was being set up by those that didn't like him in the valley. And — I'm sorry, Glen — but I hear your mother and Helen have backed him one hundred per cent. They can see no wrong in him."

"Yeah." Lateen felt exhaustion seeping into him. "If only I could prove to them what Blackstock is really like . . . "

Rosemary's eyes rounded. "You could show them this," she said gesturing at his battered body.

Lateen attempted to laugh hollowly, but pain seared him. He gasped against his nausea, "I doubt if I'd get close enough to the ranch alive to do that." Then he said, more out of curiosity than anything else, "What do you know about L. T. Spencer, girl?"

Rosemary's cheeks took on a hint of red. "He's . . . " She paused. "Recently he has started to bother me, though I try to keep out of his way. Sort of sparkin' me, I guess. I think, though, he just wants to provoke Pa into a fight, through me. That's why I've never told Pa, and I've asked those who have been with me when he has been foolin' around not to, either. But how long it can go on like that, I don't know. The truth is bound to come out sometime, though I dread it."

Lateen looked at her sharply. Here was a wise head on young shoulders. But, as she said, there was inevitably going to come the day when Jud or Henry would find out. And without doubt, the both of them would go straight for the shootist with guns. And, he knew, they would stand no chance against L. T. Spencer. In his judgement, there was a cold mankiller of the first rank.

"Well, so long as he don't do nothin' bad, try to keep it a secret as long as you can, girl," he said. "Maybe I could have a word with L. T. Spencer myself on your behalf."

Each word coated with lead, he thought.

He closed his eyes. He was so tired. He still felt appallingly weak and sore.

He let his body relax as well as he could. The problems dogging this range could wait, just a little while longer . . .

Somewhere on the edge of his hearing he thought he heard a whisper of lightly shod feet on polished boards leaving the room . . .

★ ★ ★

When he awoke Lateen found the room was dark.

Out in the valley the sounds coming in with the warm breeze wafting through the open window were familiar to him. He could hear the coyotes yipping, hear cattle lowing and bawling. They were similar to the sounds he could remember as a wild, free boy lying with Abel in their small bedroom on a clear summer's night in the cramped cabin that had been the old Double L. Those days seemed a thousand years ago now.

So it came as a big shock to hear the guns begin to crack their whiplash noise out there, too, and close. Then he heard shouting erupt below him in what he knew to be — if it hadn't been altered — was the big livingroom of the Q Lazy R. Then he heard boots running along the stoop below the window, shouts coming from farther away as well — and the boom of more guns.

Then the cry came, "They've fired the barn!"

Lateen reared up in bed, striving to ignore the pain the sudden movement ripped through his body. With agony-filled difficulty he swivelled his legs out of the bed and lowered his feet to the floor.

Gritting his teeth against his hurts he stood up, blew out the lamp by his bed and crossed to the window. Now he could see the huge barn some fifty yards from the house, gaunt in the moonlight. There were red-yellow tongues of flame licking up around the south-west corner of it.

Too, he could see the silhouettes of

what he took to be the raiding riders spreading out into the night, chased by the beginnings of spiteful gunfire from the ranch.

Then he could see men running with buckets. Others were answering the rifle shots coming in from the dark range, whose stark flame pitted bright light in the night beyond the ranch buildings.

Then he saw the tall, sinewy figure of Jud Francome running on long legs towards the trough. Behind him followed Henry, his son — more thickset than his father. Reaching the trough Jud set the wind pump working and soon it was squeaking as the night breeze caught it and spewing water into the long container.

"Get the horses out," Jud was now bawling. "And there's a load of winter hay in there, boys! We could be damn near done fer if we don't save it."

Already the screams of terrified horses were coming from inside the barn. Soon, men began leading out

145

panicked beasts. Lateen decided they must be part of the Francomes' stock of good saddle horses.

He could now see more men tumbling out of the long bunkhouse, too, down near the creek, some still in a state of half-dress. Already a bucket-chain was forming and soon water was being splashed against the barn side.

"Four men!" Jud Francome was bawling now. "Mount up. Git after those sonsofbitches!"

Though the pain searing his body caused by moving forced sweat to sheen his brow, Lateen fumbled for and found his denims. He had noticed that afternoon that they had been washed and ironed and folded neatly over the chair back near the window.

Gritting his teeth he drew the denims on. Then he pulled on his shirt over the bandages still wrapping parts of his body, then his vest. Then he found his socks and boots. Within moments he had pulled them on and was standing and stomping his boots into fitting

146

around his bruised feet. His gunbelt was there, cleaned and soaped, but no gun.

And that left him naked.

The sweat on his forehead now began to form rivulets and trickle down his still bruise-swollen face as he hobbled down the stairs into the big livingroom. The kerosene lamps were still burning down here. He could see a meal had been in progress, too, when the ruckus had started. It had been abandoned in haste. Out of cautious habit, he blew out the lamps before leaving the room.

Outside, on the stoop, he grasped one of the uprights to support him and paused to fight the pain seizing him before going down the steps and on to the hard-packed ground in front of the ranchhouse.

Rosemary came up to him from the rear of the ranchhouse. She was carrying a bucket. Her eyes became wide and round, to see him there. "Glen Lateen, get back to bed!" she demanded. "Doc Rutherford said for you to stay there for at least a week."

He stared at her with hard, blue-grey eyes. "He did, huh?" he said. "Well, just give me that bucket, Rosemary, an' I'll discount that."

As he spoke he glared around him, feeling angry about the attack. He had this feeling that it had maybe been launched because he was here. Then he returned his gaze to Rosemary. "If you want something to do, girl," he said, "git the coffee goin'."

He was surprised to see resentment flare momentarily in her eyes. He knew he could be brusque. Mary Gullet had often told him. But ignoring the reminder of that, he took the bucket from her hand and, as if she was now awed by him towering over her and by his forceful nature, she just stared at him open-mouthed.

He left her standing there.

Soon he was dipping the bucket into the trough and passing it down the line. He found long, lean Jud Francome was next to him and the rancher stared at him, partly in disbelief, before a grim smile cut his gaunt, range-browned features.

"Wondered how long it would be before thet bed got too prickly," he said then carried on with the bucket chain.

As Jud spoke Lateen became aware of the four Q Lazy R riders the rancher had ordered out moments ago sweeping past, stirring up a swirl of dust as they headed off into the moon-silvered sagebrush after the fire-raisers, their guns blazing.

But the crackle of gunfire out on the range was receding fast, the flashes already distant.

"Damn them," fumed Jud. "Why don't they stand and fight?"

Lateen found himself laughing harshly. Old Jud, as he remembered, was still capable, it seemed, of spitting hell-fire, like he knew he could when roused. It gave him heart. It looked like Blackstock had rode iron-hoofed long enough on this range. It seemed it was about to bite back.

"Guess they done what they came to do," he spat out.

But even as he spoke old Jud gasped and staggered back. In the instant he did the sound of a big rifle boomed from near the bunkhouse. Lateen knew, silhouetted against the fire old Jud had made a good target, as they all did who were here.

Made battle wary years ago, Lateen dropped prone, pulling Jud down with him into the cover of the water trough, his hurts forgotten. After telling Jud to stay where he was he began to wriggle snake-like towards the shadow of the ranchhouse, calling to the rest of the men to do the same and all the time shouting out for a gun to fit his palm.

As if to answer him, Rosemary came to the ranchhouse door.

"Glen," she yelled.

As he rolled against the stoop he looked up. As he did she tossed him

150

the long Winchester in her hand, which he caught deftly. It felt good and grim satisfaction filled him.

"Get back inside, Rosemary," he bawled, before rolling over and levelling up on the flashes coming from the bunkhouse. "You're makin' yourself a target."

But as he shouted Rosemary screamed, "Pa! Oh! Pa!"

Before Lateen could do anything to prevent her she was running down the stoop steps and towards where he had left her father, in the protection of the trough.

In a desperate attempt to cover her Lateen drove off three slugs at the gunflashes down by the bunkhouse, levering the strange gun fast, before chasing after her. When he got to her side he pushed her down brutally to the ground beside her father.

"Stay down close, girl," he bawled.

And Jud gasped, "Do as he says, Rosie!"

With that said and knowing he

could do no more here and hoping Rosemary would have the good sense not to expose herself any more, Lateen scrambled up and in a crouching run, zig-zagged towards the screen of trees near the bunkhouse.

Lead kicked dirt all round him. One hunk of hot lead hummed past his ear. But it didn't deter him. He was going to nail that bushwhacking bastard down there. He wanted like hell to come up on his rear, pin his ass to the boards and beat out of him who was behind this. But — and it bit into his gut — he already felt he knew that . . .

10

HIS breath rasping from him Lateen sprawled into the brush by the river and started to belly closer to the dark, oblong shape of the bunkhouse.

The rifle fire coming from there had gone quiet. Lateen waited. He needed a target to shoot at, a shape to move up on. Then he heard a horse being made to run flat out into the night from behind the bunkhouse, towards the ridge — towards the East Mora!

Crouching low and cursing his luck, Lateen sprinted out of cover. Reaching the far edge of the bunkhouse he could see the shadowy outline of horse and rider fading into the moon-silvered sagebrush and mesquite. The man was quirting the horse viciously, bending low and riding hard.

With angry frustration Lateen halted

and pulled the Winchester into his shoulder and fired and continued firing as fast as the lever action would allow. The detonations rang with flat, whip-lashing noise into the dark valley. He kept loading until he was finally met with a dull, metallic click. Cursing, he levered and triggered again and again, angered by the fact that the rifle was empty of bullets but only half-believing it.

Then reluctantly he lowered the rifle to his side. No doubt about it, the bird had flown. For moments he glowered into the moon-silvered night before muttering darkly and turning towards the ranchhouse.

As he approached he could see the bucket chain was in action again with the cessation of the shooting. Too, he could see they were winning the fight against the fire, which heartened him. At least one thing was being done right!

But now, the excitement gone, the awareness to his hurts came back. He suddenly felt weary again — tired and aching, until he could hardly bear the pain pulsing through his bruised body, flared up by his exertions.

And by the time he reached the ranchhouse the hurts in him were like flame licking at his body and he found he was sweating profusely again.

He could see Rosemary was still kneeling by her father, his head held in her lap. Henry, though, was leading the bucket chain, bawling encouragement and instructions where they were needed.

When Lateen reached the young woman he said,

"Well, girl?"

Rosemary turned her tear-stained face up to look at him. "Pa's hurt bad, Glen," she said.

Lateen nodded grimly. "Well, damn it, stand up, woman," he ordered, "and take this rifle. I'll need to carry Jud into the house."

Though she hesitated momentarily as if resenting his abruptness, Rosemary went on to obey without protest. But Lateen was surprised by her look. He couldn't think why, but he thought — with the look — he might have got some maybe spat reaction to his brusqueness. Mary Gullet had often complained to him that he could be too sharp — impatient, particularly with women. But that was the way he was and they'd better learn to live with that while they were around him. Anyway, couldn't the girl see Jud was doing no good out here?

He stooped, fighting back his own pain, and picked up the lanky old man. Lateen found Jud was lighter than he thought he might be, even though he was almost dead weight, unconscious as he was. Straightened and with long strides, he carried the old man towards the ranchhouse. Rosemary ran anxiously in front of him.

In the house she threw the rifle on to the long settee, lighted and picked up a kerosene lamp, then gestured to him. "In here, Glen," she said.

She led him to a bedroom and set the lamp down on the chest of drawers by the iron frame bed. It was a man's room, Lateen decided, furnished only with what a man reckoned he needed.

"On the bed," she said.

As Lateen lowered the rancher he stirred and groaned. Lateen could see blood soaked his shirt, and that the wound was high up in the shoulder. With treatment, it shouldn't be too much of a problem unless it turned nasty. Even so . . .

"Guess he needs Doc Rutherford," he said.

Rosemary nodded. "I'll get one of the hands to ride into Craddock." Then she stared at him, clearly shocked by what she saw in the pale yellow light. "But what about yourself, Glen? You look beat, too. Are *you* all right?"

He wasn't, he had to admit to himself. He felt weak, light-headed, and now the wooden floor beneath his feet felt as though it was made of soft, deep cushions that give way under his tread, unbalancing him. His limbs were trembling, too, and his knees felt as though they were turning to jelly. Clearly the effort of carrying Jud Francome had drained out what remaining strength was left in him.

"I can take care of myself," he said gruffly. "Jest you get someone heading for Craddock."

He could see that slight resentment again in her eyes at his brusqueness, but was too tired to heed it much. Some women didn't seem to want to cotton to man's straight logic at all. Yet maybe she was just naturally concerned about him, too. But really, at the moment, he didn't give a damn. For once more, shattering his masculine ego, everything was going hazy again.

Fight it as he might he was going light-headed and the room was going swimmy. And once more he felt he was being a soft, puny fool to give way to it. But that brutal dragging those Double L bastards had given him must have taken more out of him than he was allowing himself to admit to . . .

He hung on to the iron frame of the bedhead for moments before he wobbled to the floor. In that split second before unconsciousness he was lucid only long enough to hear Rosemary's startled cry,

"Glen! I told you!"

★ ★ ★

When he came to, Lateen found he was in bed once more and that the sun was pouring its hot light in long shafts through the open window.

He sat up sharply. Again the pain hit him — though it wasn't so bad this time. And, with an odd perverseness, it even caused him to smile grimly to himself. Now it only felt as though he'd been through a hay tosser instead of an ore crusher.

His grim humour set him chuckling to himself but he soon gave it up. To laugh — hell, now that really did hurt!

He screwed up his face and looked around him. His clothes were again folded neatly over the back of the chair under the window. Seeing them he edged gingerly out of bed and grunting with the hurts the exertion caused him, he pulled on his denims.

As he did his body started its burning again where it was rashed and cut, but, he realized, it was also beginning to itch, too. He decided that if he could get to the trough, sink into it, he would maybe douse this burning, drive it away . . .

His need for that comfort fixed itself uppermost in his mind and he went downstairs. On the way out he looked in on Jud Francome but found he was sleeping. Nobody was in the big living room either, but he could smell ham and eggs cooking and it made him realize how ravenously hungry he was. However, the hunger would have to wait. When he had negotiated the stoop steps, he moved across the bare expanse of ground there to the trough.

He gasped at its coldness as he dropped into it, but rejoiced, too, in the effect it had on his body.

Then he sighed and closed his eyes and lay soaking.

"Do we have to tie you down, Glen Lateen?" the voice demanded. He knew it was Rosemary's.

He cocked open an eye. He looked up and smiled at her. The sun was behind her, her body splitting the rays, blocking them — preventing them reaching his eyes.

"Mebbe so," he said. He broadened his smile to a grin. "I smelled ham and eggs on the way here."

"You could of had them in bed," she said.

"Damn it," he said. "Anybody would think I was an invalid."

"According to Doc Rutherford, you are, or should be," she countered hotly. "But he said — after last night — you're maybe too ornery for that."

"He been here?" Lateen stared up.

She nodded. "Left maybe half an

hour ago after fixin' up Pa. He was yawning his head off and cursing the free use of firearms on this range and the people behind them. He looked in on you, too. Said all you needed was rest — plenty of rest — for the next few days."

"Your Pa's wound . . . ?" Lateen said then.

"Bullet went through after glancing off the shoulderblade. Missed the vital parts." Rosemary added with clear relief, "He'll be laid up for a spell, but he'll be fine."

Thankful satisfaction filled Lateen, for he had the vague feeling this raid could have been mounted on the Q Lazy R because he was here. But the idea was pure speculation.

"Well, that's somethin'," he said.

Lateen drew his big, bruise-covered frame up and stepped out of the trough and stood dripping water on to the hoof-churned ground around him. Looking down at his white upper torso, made more stark by the bright sunlight, he could see the great purple bruises, cuts and rashes covering his body.

"Does the doc know how I got like this?" he said.

"No," Rosemary said. "Nobody does, properly. But I reckon he can guess what happened, bein' a medical man. Only I know you accused the Double L riders of it."

"Accused hell," rasped Lateen. "They did it." Then he narrowed his eyes. "I've been thinkin', too, the business last night was maybe because you took me in."

Rosemary raised dark eyebrows. "Doubt it," she said. "L. T. Spencer and Horst Blackstock, and the border trash they ride with, have been making threats aplenty against the Q Lazy R, claiming we're stealing their beef. Looks like, with the raid, they've decided to come clean out of the woodwork."

Lateen pulled at his bruised face. "Even so, it could have got back to the Double L I'm here."

Rosemary looked a little bemused,

skeptical even. "But surely Helen and your Ma would be wanting to know how you got like this if it had," she said. "They certainly wouldn't be sending a shooting party."

Though it hurt him to say it Lateen muttered, with slow despair, "On that score I'm beginning to have my doubts, Rosemary."

With the comment he brought himself up sharply, shocked by the bitter reservations growing in him. So much so he felt he should try to qualify what he meant.

"Not maybe Helen," he said. He compressed his lips. "But Ma?" His stare turned cold as well as a little sad. "I shot down Palau, sure, because he left me no choice. But because Palau's wife is niece to Blackstock, it seemed that no-account trash was more important to Ma than me. My side of the shooting wasn't even asked for."

Lateen sighed, feeling defeated by his doubts. But he squared his big shoulders, shook his head which was shaggy with long, wet, uncut locks. But he still felt bitterness at the reception he had received at the Double L. "Damn it, I have to try an' get through to them."

Though he saw sympathy in Rosemary's eyes she said, "Oh, Glen, why did you have to turn to mankilling? Helen often said if you had stayed on at the ranch after the war things could have been so different."

Lateen nodded, though he vaguely felt it was a woman taking woman's side. "Well, it's all water under the bridge, Rosemary," he said. "In the eyes of God an' Ma I'm still just a no good mankiller."

Rosemary shook her young head. She still looked bemused, almost tearful. "I just don't know what to believe any more," she said. "I find it just too awful that people can be like this."

Lateen looked towards the house and saw Henry Francome coming out of the ranchhouse. He came down the stoop steps with a rolling gait to his slightly bowed legs. And it immediately struck up memories in Lateen. As children he and Abel had played long hours with Henry on those very steps. They had even gone off to war together, all of them bushy-tailed and full of hell.

"Glen," Henry said, smiling warmly as he approached. "How you feelin'?"

Lateen gazed at the stocky, thickset man standing before him. Henry still had a round, honest face and still had that faint, shy smile he remembered had always lingered socially on his generous lips.

"I'm bringin' trouble on you, Henry," he said abruptly. "If you could vittle me and fit me up with some guns and a horse I'll be ridin'. Before I leave this valley I got some scores to settle."

Henry nodded knowingly. "Well, first you ain't troublin' us," he said. "An' second, I got scores to settle, too. Rosemary says you believe it's Horst Blackstock who's behind all this." He nodded. "Well, I'm coming round to believin' that myself since that God-awful business over at Jim Wayne's place."

Lateen pursed his lips. "Well, I ain't certain of nothin' yet. But I'd like you to give me a few days before you start your own campaign. As a Lateen it galls me to think the Double L may be responsible for what's goin' on, an' for attackin' good friends like yourself."

Henry appeared to be a little flattered by that but also uncertain, too. "Well, thank you, Glen," he said. "But I think we should tackle this together. It's not only us, it's the whole valley. Some are plain scared, others riled up. It's gettin' to be some of the smaller homesteaders and ranchers are thinkin' of movin' after what happened to Jim Wayne and Barret Tucker, him bein' a U.S. lawman, an all."

Lateen nodded. "Yeah, I can understand a family man feeling like that. But there is the chance that Blackstock, L. T. Spencer and those gunslinging trash ridin' with them maybe think, because of my reputation, I'm out of the way dead now and won't be around to bother them. That could give me a chance to work quiet. I got to try an' get in touch with Abel, find out if he knows what's really goin' on."

Henry's brown gaze levelled, keen and sharp, though a little embarrassed, as if he was loath to say his next words. "Well, Abel ain't the man he was, Glen," he said. "He ain't even leanin' on God too much these days. Since Blackstock and his gunnies moved in, he seems to have gone downhill more'n ever. An' that leg plagues him somethin' terrible sometimes. Over the years fightin' it, it seems to have worn all the spunk out of him."

Lateen nodded, eyelids narrow. "I know about the bottle, Henry," he said softly. "But, I don't think Abel's played out yet. Even so, can I count on you if I need you?"

Lateen could see Henry's eyes were sharp and keen and sincere as they met his own level gaze. "Hell, from right now, Glen, you on'y have to whistle," he said. He nodded towards the house. "My pa lies shot in there. We're losin' more beef than we can afford. Be sure, the Q Lazy R and its resources are available whenever you want them. I just hope what's goin' on ain't nothin' to do with your ma, or Helen, is all."

"Well, I can't argue with that," Lateen said heavily. "But we still got to prove the Double L's at the back of the play in the valley." He added, "It may be the stuff with me is just personal — "

Henry looked doubtful. "Perhaps," he said. "But — and I'm sorry to say it, Glen — I figure Helen an' your ma are wide-eyed gone on Blackstock, enough to not be able to see straight no more. Though your ma did a fine job on the ranch through the bad years, Blackstock's expertise since then has built it up to what it is now. But there is a black greed in that man. He jest wants more."

"Yeah, I'm figurin' you're right, Henry," Lateen said. "But with the law the way I've heard it is over at River Falls we have to have it watertight, or see Horst Blackstock dead. And in the killin' department, I've nothin' to lose and plenty of expertise. And, it seems, in Texas I'll wear that brand to my grave."

"It ain't right you shoulderin' the valley's problems, Glen," Henry said. "I've got the feelin' you've left the wild days behind, despite killin' August Palau."

Lateen levelled his blue-grey stare on to the man before him. "Well, you're right on that score, Henry," he said, "but it looks like the troubles on this range have been done in the name of the Double L, an' because of the name of the family that owns it, that makes it my business. Just give me two days to try and work somethin' out."

"But you ain't fit!" protested Henry. Rosemary, who had been listening intently, butted in. "Henry's right," she said. "Leave it to the Q Lazy R'til you're well, Glen."

Lateen turned on Rosemary. "I could sure use some of those ham and eggs, girl," he said. He felt that was maybe more diplomatic than he usually was, and Mary Gullet would have been pleased with him.

Rosemary stared and compressed her attractive lips. "Men! They think a woman can't think straight, that all they are here for is to fill their bellies and bear their children!"

She stalked off.

Henry said, "Whooooheeee! You got her spittin' fire now."

Lateen allowed a grim smile to come to his lips. "That girl's got spirit," he said. "She'll make somebody a fine wife. Well, Henry . . . guns, a hoss an' some time?"

Henry Francome nodded reluctantly. "You got it, Glen," he said. "But keep in touch."

On the high central ridge splitting the Mora Valley into a U shape, and away from the gap taking the trail to the Double L, Lateen threaded his way along its near top — through the tall, dark rocks scarring the skyline. Occasionally he gazed at the valley spreading away each side, shimmering under the blazing sun. To his right, on the East Mora range, he could see, mingled amongst the longhorns there, the white faces of Herefords distributed throughout the Double L herds. And like dust-clouded blobs, he could see groups of cowboys moving amongst them, chivvying groups to fresh pastures. From where he was Lateen could see the impressive sprawl of Double L ranchhouse. The mansion was — though distant — still an imposing sight. He wondered what Helen and Ma were doing . . .

Grim-faced at the thought of them, Lateen hitched in the worn saddle he had been loaned. He wasn't here for the sightseeing, or daydreaming . . .

Near the more desolate part of the ridge, where it began to meld with the northern foothills, Lateen pulled rein a hundred yards from the cave he and Abel had rendezvoused in as boys, remembering the silly code they used to fool their Ma: Banka Wallanka Ballantee. In the brush he tied the Q Lazy R buckskin mare he rode, drew the loaned Winchester from its saddle holster and crept forward.

Maybe Abel had left him something — a note, maybe — when he had not found him here two days ago . . .

But when he entered the small cavern his gut knotted. Abel was in an awkward, crumpled position on the cave floor. Lateen could see he had been shot through the back, twice. One shot had blown apart Abel's spine, the other had entered the back of his head. God knew what Abel's face would look like . . .

Angry mourning already in him,

Lateen bent over him. Abel was stiff. He had been here some time. Now hurting deeply with the discovery, Lateen rolled his brother over.

He turned away abruptly at the sight of what was left of Abel's face. But when he returned his gaze he could see there was a piece of paper clasped in Abel's left hand. It had obviously been hidden by his body and clearly missed by Abel's assassin. A pencil was clasped and broken in Abel's right hand. Had he heard something, tried to scribble something . . . ?

Though repulsed by the necessity, Lateen knew he would possibly have to break Abel's fingers to get the note out of his hand. But it could be that important. Scoured by the necessity and brutality of the task, Lateen's bruised and scarred face set in severe lines.

"Forgive me, Abel," he said. But he found he could not keep the tremble out of his voice.

When he straightened from his grisly

task he smoothed out the paper he had retrieved. What was on it puzzled him. Just two words.

Helen is . . .

That was all. Lateen stared. A frown formed on his brow. *Helen is . . .* what? A target?

And what about the murdering skunk that had backshot Abel?

Lateen stared at the body. He could see Abel didn't even have a gun. No cartridge belt. Nothing. Then Lateen remembered that bleak day he had returned to the ranch twelve years ago after the war, before he had been banished from it by his unforgiving mother. Abel had not worn a gun then. Nor had Lateen seen one on him during their brief encounter at the Double L four days ago. He could only assume that Abel had maybe long since forsaken the use of guns because of his war experiences and his vowed commitment to God after.

And in Lateen's book that made the killing even more loathsome. Cold, brutal murder had clearly been committed here. There was no doubt about that.

No spark of mercy for whoever had done this glowed in Lateen's eyes as he drew from his own gunbelt the Colt Henry Francome had loaned him. It was a well-balanced Frontier model. Lateen had got the feel of it quickly. A number of practice draws from leather had satisfied him even though it was a strange gun — the change to it had lost him nothing in speed.

And for years he hadn't known this overwhelming, pulsing urge to kill that now flared up in him. He doubted if he'd ever really had it. It'd always been a case of kill or be killed with him, self-defence. He had never got any kick out of it. And he had never seriously looked for trouble, either, despite his hellraising propensities. It had always seemed to find him. But now this would be a matter of bitter revenge for a well-loved brother.

And that was a different matter entirely.

11

IT was as if instinct had driven him.

When he got to within half a mile of the Double L ranch buildings, Lateen tied up the Q Lazy R buckskin mare in a stand of cottonwoods by a small creek. His heart still heavy within him at finding his brother murdered, he hauled the stiff body from the saddle. The horse again shied nervously for, from the first, it hadn't liked the task of carrying the cadaver.

Revenge and the fact that he was his brother had driven Lateen to withstand the smell of decomposition already emanating from Abel. And he had let out what body gas there was in his brother before he had started on the long walk to the ranch.

Now he would have to drag Abel to the ranch. What he was about to do with his brother, he acknowledged to himself, would be considered ghoulish by some, but personally, he viewed it as a grim necessity. He had to let them know they were being watched, that they were being rumbled.

Even so, in the cloudy dark of that Texas night that toned down the shine of the moon, coming down off the ridge, he had constantly asked forgiveness from Abel, his own revulsion at what he was doing persistent.

He wanted Blackstock, or that murdering scum L. T. Spencer, to sweat when they saw Abel, wonder who could have towed the corpse down here, place it onto the ground in front of the big mansion and leave it there in the full view of all. He wanted Ma and Helen to see it, too, to make them take their blinkers off, see what was going on under their noses, make them see what Blackstock or Spencer were capable of. For he had no doubt that those two were in some way responsible for Abel's death.

178

And particularly, he wanted to make Ma see through her uncompromising, high-nosed morality and comprehend what she had encouraged here.

Lateen calmed himself down. Bitterness would get him nowhere. The facts seemed to be that Blackstock had too strong a hold on Helen and Ma for them to accept that he could ever possibly be involved in anything bad. The women, from what he could judge, seemed ready to accept Blackstock's word on everything. He'd heard they could be like that . . .

Lateen compressed his lips. No, it would call for calm nerves and steady thinking here — not the mixture of hate and remorse and mourning that seethed in him and almost blinded him at the moment.

Even so, it was a puzzle as to who could have followed Abel to their childhood hideout and there killed him. But — and it generated slow cold anger in Lateen — he reckoned he already knew the answer to that. He had noticed L. T. Spencer had been made more than a little curious by Abel's called codeword to him when they had been escorting him from the ranch to be tortured, four days ago. He could maybe have kept a close eye on Abel and . . .

But it was all speculation.

Troubled by his thoughts, and towing Abel by his collar, Lateen moved with short sidesteps towards the Double L. And as he did he stared occasionally at the night sky. Dark clouds drifted across the moon and stars; coyotes howled, deep in the East Mora.

It was also late and, as he drew close, Lateen found the ranchhouse and outbuildings were mostly black and silent. Only one lamp burned on the wall next to the big ranchhouse door and one light showed in one of the large downstairs rooms, but he could nót see anybody moving about in it.

Panting and sweating with his exertions and slightly nauseated by Abel's decomposing smell, Lateen came to rest against the barn wall closest to the house. He felt drained and still weak from the pain and loss of blood his murderous dragging still caused him.

Gently he laid Abel's stiff body to the ground and wiped the sweat from his brow. He peered across the worn, open space to the mansion intently, his ears straining to pick up any noise. And, coming from the direction of the central ridge, he picked up the muted drumming of hooves. And as the rider drew close, even in this dark, Lateen could not mistake the big frame of Horst Blackstock in the saddle.

At the steps leading to the ranch terrace, Blackstock slid off the horse's back, undid the girth, walked up the steps and dumped the saddle over the balustrade-like railings fronting the terrace. Then he led the horse to the corral and beat its rump, sending it trotting into the cedarwood pen, towards the trough.

But it was as Blackstock came into the light of the lamp on the house wall, making hollows in his face, that Lateen's memory was jolted and he finally nailed the event that had plagued him since first meeting Blackstock in the Schooner Saloon, and that was — *where he had seen the bastard before*.

He was Miles Foster! A bloody, rogue *Federal* officer, but in the Quantrill mould. It all came flooding back. That night during the war when Lateen had been part of the small garrison protecting Genner's Ford in east Texas. The union guerrillas, led by Blackstock, had struck it without warning, sacking the houses and its bank while torching the whole town. Some forty of the citizens had been killed mercilessly, many more injured, in an orgy of blood-letting.

At the memory of that bloody night, Lateen narrowed his eyelids. How *he* had got out of that bloodbath with his life was still a mystery to him. But he had and he had seen Foster briefly — silhouetted as he now was in the light of that lamp, but then the light had been from the angry fires of the burning town.

Blackstock was different now, certainly — older and more full of face. But it was Foster. No doubt about it. And there had grown a mystery around him, too. About mid 1863 Foster had disappeared from the scene, some said a rich man, some said finally rundown and killed. Several took credit for that, but there had never been any real proof.

Lateen's hand went for his Colt instinctively. If for no other reason, he wanted to avenge the destruction of Genner's Ford. But he stayed his hand. *Not yet.*

He watched Blackstock cross the terrace, open the big door and go into the house. With eyes the colour of cold steel, Lateen's gaze searched across the windows of the mansion. Then he saw Blackstock come into the room with the light in it. To his surprise he saw Helen rise from the deep chair by the fire to greet him. She hadn't been visible until now. The two started talking animatedly. Conflicting emotions immediately stirred in Lateen. Besides anger, the meeting aroused his curiosity. What *could* Helen see in that murdering renegade? What could they possibly have to talk about? And surely she should have seen through him by now?

Compelled by his inquisitiveness, he went forward after he had placed Abel tenderly but conspicuously in the centre of the worn space before the ranchhouse. He tiptoed to the window. The lower section of the sash window had been opened to allow the cool night air to enter the room.

"Glen's still alive?" Helen was saying. Her voice sounded angry and surprised. "After all that, they didn't kill him?"

The words brought Lateen up, though he was hardly able to comprehend them. Through the gently waving net curtains his astonished gaze could see Helen's breasts were heaving with emotion. She was pacing the floor. Her voice was full of disbelief.

Lateen now found his gut was knotting. *She knew*? Jesus, God, what was she saying? What was he hearing?

Blackstock was nodding. "Doc Rutherford told Charley behind the bar of the Schooner Saloon that he had seen your damned brother this very morning at the Q Lazy R, sleeping as peaceful as a babe. And from what he'd been told he was getting stronger by the day."

His emotions riven with disbelief and despair Lateen stared at Helen. She was looking at her husband. Her eyes were stricken. Her hand went trembling to her mouth.

"I keep telling you, he isn't my brother!" she shrieked. "Ma — *that woman* — exploded that myth last year when I asked about the will and she told me she had adopted me because, before they had left Alabama, she had been told she couldn't have children. And because I wasn't kin, the ranch would never go to me while Glen and

Abel were alive. *I'm not a Lateen*, you hear?"

Stunned, Lateen swung round, his mind a jumble of numbed incredulity. He sagged against the ranchhouse wall. Helen — not his sister? He felt as though he had been put on a medieval rack, the pictures of which he had seen in the history books he had read as a boy. Like that terrible thing he felt as though his own emotions had been put there and torn apart by Helen's disclosures.

He turned and stared through the window again, at the scene in the room. Blackstock was shrugging. "OK," he said. "You're not kin. What the hell? The thing is, he's still alive. He's survived."

Lateen watched Helen look up from the fire she turned to stare at after her outburst. Her eyes were hard and steady — but not Lateen eyes, as he had always thought they were. Her reply came in, sharp and cutting as sharded glass.

"I wanted him shot quickly, cleanly," she said harshly. "Not tortured. I — I still feel something for Glen, despite . . . "

"And I respected that," Blackstock said indignantly. "It was L. T. Spencer's idea. I coded to him I wanted him shot. I knew nothin' about what we heard — that business with the dragging, and the mule hide — and I'll deal with it when I see him. But you know how close L.T. an' Palau grew to be. I guess he felt extra bad about August's death. Spencer once told me about how he'd seen a man die like that once. It had been in Mexico. Maybe he wanted to make Glen suffer for killin' Palau."

"He's scum," Helen said bitterly. Lateen could see her blue-grey eyes were glittering and deadly in the lamplight. "The sooner we can finish with him, and the rest of them, the better."

Lateen saw an almost half-sneer come to Blackstock's thick lips. "L.T.'s scum?" he said. "My God." He chuckled wryly. "Yeah, well, you know, honey, when I first met you and for sometime after, I would never have taken you for what you've turned out to be, either. But they do say the female of the species can be the most deadly when crossed. An', by God, I've fast come round to believing that. But you got to appreciate what slot you're sittin' in. Fact is now, honey, you ain't no better than L.T., though it grieves me to say it, you bein' my wife. And because of that, we don't go around name-callin' our own kind."

As if warming to his task Blackstock levelled his gaze on Helen. He said, "You know, you could have left Glen in Wyoming — and should have, like I advised. You should never have told your Ma — "

"She's not my mother!" Helen shouted.

Blackstock's dark eyes studied her. "Yeah, well you shouldn't have told Miz Lateen that Glen was still alive, a ranch foreman and almost weaned off his gun-totin' ways — "

"I didn't know about not being kin then!" Helen spat.

Blackstock continued as if he hadn't been interrupted. Lateen thought he sounded almost mocking. "Well, it sure put a double loop on your ambitions, didn't it, when your *guardian* insisted, because of that, that Glen should take over the running of the Double L when she died — seein' as how Abel has turned out to be such a lush."

Astounded by the revelations coming at him, Lateen stared numbly at Helen through the gently waving net curtains. As if wrenched from him, leaving an open, bleeding sore that would never heal, he found the tender feelings he had always held for Helen were flowing from him.

She had wanted him killed?

He continued to stare. Now all he could see were the hard lines on her face, the coldness in her eyes, the look of what appeared to be bitter, disillusioned frustration.

As he watched, Helen started to pace the floor again, clearly agitated by Blackstock's words. Then she paused at a silver box on a round, gleaming mahogany table in the middle of the big room. She took out a long panatella and lit it with a sulphur match.

Then she said, "I had expected the sanctimonious bitch I have called mother for thirty four years to have died before Glen arrived. I wanted Glen to take over legally, as required in the will, to satisfy lawyer Mason we were on the level, then have him bushwhacked. The way we've got things stirred up in the valley, we could easily blame rustlers for his death — anybody, in fact. We'd be clean. I suppose a lot of people would even say Glen had finally got his come-uppance . . . "

As she spoke Helen kept on pacing. She waved the hand holding the panatella in the air. "Well, what's happened has just changed the plans a little," she said. "In a way it was fortunate Glen shot down Palau, fortunate it renewed Ma's revulsion for his mankilling ways — enough to send him packing once more. And maybe some good has come out of it. The discovery of the fact Glen still is a killer has about finished her, sent her to the bed she's lying in now. Doc Rutherford gives her a week at the most."

There Helen paused, her look twisted with bitterness. "You know, the irony is," she said, "though she's never admitted it, the old fool still loves Glen deeply, always has. But she's as bullheaded stubborn as he is."

Lateen found he was having difficulty holding onto and accepting all that was coming at him. Remorse began to lash him. He watched Blackstock grin, sending murderous anger through him. It looked cynical.

Blackstock said, "Yeah, she even told me she has absolute belief when she's dead that he'll be back when he learns of his inheritance and that someday the Lord will take him under His wing and redeem him and that the Double L will remain in Lateen hands forever."

Helen stopped pacing. Her stare had changed again. It became narrow, evil. "Yes, and he's still alive," she said. "And, while he is and if he lives up to his reputation, he's our biggest danger — for he'll be back, never fear. I know Glen well enough to know he'll never let up."

"That's why I had the men hit the Q Lazy R last night, to kill that reputation before it could cause us any more trouble, but they loused it up," Blackstock grumbled. "But I tell you, I reckon one thing is certain now: Lateen knows how he stands at the Double L. I should have let L.T. go on the job — take care of it. He wouldn't have turned tail. Bayer said he'd seen Glen, up on his feet and gunning. He said he'd tried for him, but had hit Jud Francome instead."

Helen stared. She said scornfully, "And you said Doc Rutherford had claimed he wouldn't pull through."

Blackstock looked resentful. "And so

he did, when he first tended him." Then he sniggered. "He felt I should know, so that I could tell you and you could fetch him. You should have done."

Helen ignored the jibe. "And now you say he's OK?"

Blackstock nodded. "That's what Doc Rutherford told Charley."

Helen angrily ground out the panatella in a convenient ashtray. "Well, from tomorrow I want every gunslinging scum we've got out on the range," she said. "I want Glen found and killed on sight."

Blackstock's dark eyes studied her. "Woooooheee," he breathed. "I sure found a she-cat when I found you. Makes me wonder sometimes where I fit in, and for how long . . ."

Lateen watched Helen's eyes soften to the tenderness he knew could be there when she looked at her husband. "You know where you stand with me, Horst," she said. "You gave me my boy, James; you gave me love. And

193

we're two of a kind. You know, I've had little love in my life, except maybe from Glen. And that, whatever you may think, makes this real hard for me. But it won't stop me. The Double L is mine. I've earned my right to it. Glen's earned nothing and because of that he must die."

Lateen found an intense sadness filling him. Yes, he had known plenty of tender feeling from Helen and had reciprocated it. Now she was giving the love she had to Blackstock. It must sure have been one hell of a blow to her system to learn what Ma considered was Helen's true place at the Double L. To be told she had virtually no place in the hierarchy here until he and Abel were dead must have been devastating. Ma had allowed the hard carapace she had formed around herself to ward off the hurts of life to take almost all loving feeling out of her, to confront Helen with such a brutal declaration. But for Helen to turn out to be the woman she now was . . .

Pain snarled up Lateen's insides.

He watched Blackstock cross to her, watched him take her in his arms and kiss her tenderly. And Helen melted to him, sighing as she did. "Let's go to bed, Horst," she said. "It's been some time."

12

IN the shadows outside the ranch-house window Lateen turned and flattened himself against the wall. He felt bewildered, torn by all the emotions that were writhing inside him.

As the lamplight in the room faded behind him and darkness closed in on the terrace and he heard the room door close, he found his whole body was shaking. He found he could not bring himself to believe what he had heard. But now the bloodied, pencilled words on the paper in Abel's dead hand began to make ghastly sense. *Helen is* . . . *behind it all?*

Then a further, awful possibility came to him. *Had Helen, in fact, killed Abel?*

The enormity of the prospect caused Lateen to roll his head back and forth against the warm boards to try and deny it. God, no. That was too terrible to contemplate. But she did know the hideout and she might have heard Abel call the codeword to him. She knew what it meant. Abel was in her way, too, being a Lateen . . .

He found it had become hard to control his breathing and that his anguish was causing the blood to pound in his temples. He found he still did not want to believe what he had heard, wanted to deny his own ears. But Helen had made it clear that when she had heard that the ranch would not be hers, as she had obviously longed for and hoped it would be, and that she wasn't even a Lateen, it had been as though all the pent-up fires of the dark side that was in all humanity had been released within her.

He closed his eyes to try and shut the appalling revelations out. It must have flipped her already crippled mind.

For being older and 'big sister' she had always been respected and loved by both him and Abel. And he had always assumed she was kin, as she clearly had. She had, however, always been dominated by Ma and had allowed it to be so. That wasn't a Lateen trait at all, he decided. And he should have suspected it.

Lateen stared into the dark night. But then had come the piledriver for Helen, that she was not kin and would never inherit while he and Abel were alive. Maybe she had taken Ma's bullying all those years with just that prospect in mind, he and Abel turning out the way they had. She had perhaps originally married Blackstock to see the ranch supervised profitably when it became hers, the Lateen line maintained through their issue — as James already was. Maybe, he speculated, she had waited with that hope in mind — prepared to live under the regime of piety and tyranny that existed here under Ma until the day when Ma died and Helen would become mistress of the Double L. Yes, all those possible high dreams she'd had — destroyed by that one terrible revelation.

The turmoil his emotions were in tore at him. Everything was maybes, if onlys. Maybe all this was because he had not stayed after the war. He had rode away instead of buckling down . . .

Lateen found his terrible remorse was almost physical. It was perhaps he that had brought them all to this. Maybe Ma would have softened if she had had him to lean on, hand over the reins to. But it was all gone, never to be retrieved. Poor, twisted Helen. Poor, inadequate Abel.

Still reeling with the emotions the revelations had aroused in him Lateen limped down the terrace steps to stand swaying in the night, numbed, sick and heart-torn.

But the harsh cry from his left swiftly drove his misery out.

"Hell! Lateen!"

Lateen swung round, already driving his hand towards the butt of his Colt.

As he lifted his iron, his thumb was cocking the hammer in the same fluid movement. In the gloom he could see it was L. T. Spencer he faced.

Then, thundering into his ears, the guns crashed out. Lateen saw Spencer's face become a vivid mask in the powder-flashes. Then Lateen felt Spencer's lead tug at a strand of his long, dark hair, which hung out from under his jammed-down hat. More lead hummed past him — close.

But already Lateen could see L. T. Spencer was reeling sideways and pitching back, his eyes staring in disbelief, blood already smearing his shirt. As the shootist hit the hard-packed ground a long sigh escaped him and air hissed out of the hole in his chest. L. T. Spencer giggled once, inanely, before he died.

Lateen, now taut, eyes blazing, his senses made vividly alert by the sudden life or death situation he had been plunged into, stared immediately out into the darkness around him, but nobody else was in the near vicinity.

Though he could still hear the faint sound of gunfire echoing along the ridge hidden by the night, the night sounds gradually stilled to become silent again. Then lights shining through windows began to pierce the dark. Shouts were being raised.

Shocked out of his numbness by the action just gone, Lateen plunged into the brush and began running for the Q Lazy R buckskin mare he had left tethered in the sage. By the time he reached her his breathing was harsh and fast and rasping out of him. He swung up into the loaned saddle.

In grim silence he cut the mare across the rump with a hard hand and sent her plunging into the dark night of the East Mora Valley.

Three miles on he turned her up into the foothills.

He went deep into them before he halted on a flat, high point and waited for morning. But the events of the night wouldn't leave him.

L. T. Spencer's death mattered nothing to him. He was scum that wanted killing. It was debt paid. They had matched ability and he, Lateen, had won. End.

But in one terrible ten minute spell of revelation down there the position here in the valley had been revealed to him, and Helen's possible death sentence when justice was brought — being so deeply implicated in it — was heart-rending to him. Even so — more immediately — was, soon Blackstock's border scum would be combing the range for him and he could be dead.

One possibility to consider would be to go to the Q Lazy R, ask for help. But that would only implicate the Francomes more. Already Jud had paid the price for siding him. And at base, this was a Lateen problem that had to be solved by Lateens.

Now sitting there on this rocky lookout ledge staring at the dark maw that was the Mora Valley below him, Lateen wrung his hands in anguish. He didn't want to face the fact of Helen's involvement and its possible outcome. It was a too-evil dilemma. But face it he must.

Then, realizing he hadn't eaten since morning, he found some beef sandwiches which Rosemary Francome had stuffed into the saddlebags before he left the Q Lazy R. He ate with no appetite, taking sips of tepid water with the meal.

And as he ate the deep dark of false dawn gave way to true dawn and yellow light cut a pale scar across the eastern horizon before the sun sent rays speeding across the East Mora and spreading long shadows from the ridge across the western part of the valley to his right.

Now he could see the Francome place, the buildings sitting like small grey-blue boxes on the range in the distance. Smoke was starting to rise from the stone chimney of the ranchhouse. Down on the East Mora, the Double L mansion was coming alive, too. He could also distinguish other ranches and holdings in the valley — farming or grazing the less fertile lands — but still, with hard work, had been made fruitful, but was now threatened by Blackstock's and Helen's greed.

Though the dwellings were several miles away, with the aid of the hunting glass he always kept in his possibles, he could see Double L riders fanning out like specks into the sage flats. They were clearly searching for his sign. And it wasn't long before a hand found the spot he had selected to tie up his horse last night. The puncher turned his mount and spurred it towards the ranchhouse, sending dust churning up behind him like a bright yellow banner in the sun's rays. He also saw smoke rise from a pointed-up gun, then heard very faint cracks. The rider was telling the other seekers he had found something.

In his 'scope Lateen could also pick out the bed of the dried-up

Whitewater river running from the mountains north. And it immediately set him thinking — as a rancher. If boreholes were sunk, pumps installed, water could still be reached, maybe the Whitewater was trapped in some underground reservoir?

In any event Jim Wayne's death was just a vicious attack by warped men, the water in Fisher's Creek maybe not needed, even if it would be enough. Surely Helen hadn't sanctioned it. Lateen clung to the hope it had been L. T. Spencer acting on his own initiative. He recalled Helen's reaction when he had told of Jim Wayne's lynching. It had seemed one of genuine revulsion.

He tore his thoughts away. The men down there were numerous, busy around the ranchhouse. Through the glass, at this distance, he could just pick out their form and movements, but little else. He certainly could not identify anybody, but he could see Abel's dead body had been removed from the space in front of the ranchhouse.

But even after a night of trying to come to terms with it all, Lateen found his emotions had yet to calm down.

What he had to do and how he would do it still hadn't resolved itself in him. One time, because of Helen's involvement, during the long dark night now behind him, he'd had a strong urge to ride on, leave the ranch and the valley to its own destiny. To know Helen was head-deep in the problems besetting this range, and to have to confront it, was a chore he still could hardly bring himself to face.

But then, seeing the swinging body of Jim Wayne had haunted him. There was, too, the bloody hole that had once been Abel's face he had stared into when he had turned his brother's stiff body over in the cave yesterday. There was Jud Francome with the bad wound to his shoulder. There was Barret Tucker, found dead on the trail. Could all this be laid at the Double L's door? From what he had

206

heard last night, he had little doubt.

His heart, heavy as a lump of lead within him, he watched the group of riders come running out from the Double L and head towards where he had tethered his horse last night.

He stiffened and rose. It was about to start. He felt before the end of this day the destiny of the whole of the Mora Valley was going to be sealed. And with cold certainty he knew where his duty lay, like it or not. What was happening here in the Mora could only be laid at the door of the Lateen family. *His family*. And he couldn't allow the name to be besmirched any longer. Not by Helen, not by Ma, not by anybody . . .

From here on, it all had to be purged clean.

Then he turned his 'scope west and saw the group of riders beating a trail from the Q Lazy R. He could not distinguish who was heading them yet. They were heading for the ridge, right into the path of the riders coming from the Double L following his trail with slow patience.

He reared up, grim light coming to his iron grey eyes. Knowing the mood that would be prevailing at the Double L, and the Q Lazy R, more death could bloody this land very soon. But to warn the Q Lazy R riders he would have to expose himself.

But he knew he had to do it.

13

URGENTLY Lateen got up and sprinted to where he had left the buckskin mare on a short rope in the rocks — to crop the sweet grass there. Ignoring the aches in his body, he prepared the horse for the trail.

Somehow, as he had decided, he had to get to the Q Lazy R riders before the Double L horsemen did, if only to warn them there could be gun trouble. But he was surprised by the size of the group of Q Lazy R riders. He had got to know a few of them during his brief convalescence there but most of these men were strangers to him. And why they were actually riding this way had him feeling curious.

He guided the horse down off the top of the butte he had been sitting on for most of the night. Soon he lost sight of the Q Lazy R riders, as he expected he would do, but he calculated his line meticulously and aimed his horse toward the most possible point of interception and threaded through the rocks.

After fifteen minutes of brisk riding he was where he wanted to be — but he wasn't ready for the deadly hum of lead that went fizzing hotly past his cheekbone nor the crack of the rifle accompanying it a split second after. However he was already moving when two more shots, clearly levered in fast, sent dust spurting off the rocks behind him, again missing him by a hair's breadth.

He sent the startled buckskin plunging into the rocks. And once in cover Lateen dropped out of the saddle, tugging his Winchester from its saddle scabbard as he did. Then he ran back, found cover and began to scan the skyline above him, his eyelids narrow. The dark, jagged line of rocks showed nothing except a wisp of dust that still lingered on the almost still air.

The bushwhacker would surely want to remain up there to keep above him, Lateen assumed, drawing on his own experience in such matters. And it was an odds-on certainty that the bushwhacker would not remain where he had been, his attempted killing bungled. No, if he was one of the border scum riding for the Double L, Lateen reckoned he would be professional enough to have moved by now. But which way?

Lateen tightened his grip on the stock of the big rifle, licked his suddenly dry lips. His steely stare raked the jumbled rocks. It was hellish country to be in to have this situation jumped on you.

Again a suggestion of disturbed dust rose, fifty yards along the rock-line off to his right. He brought his rifle into his shoulder. His eyes stung, felt as if they were filled with hot grit because he had been holding them open for so long, forgotten in the tenseness. He blinked twice to lubricate them, all the time keeping his gaze intently searching the area he had seen movement.

The top of a black stetson showed above the rock line this time — just for a moment, before it went again. Lateen crouched closer to the rock he was against. No shooting — not yet. He'd lived by the old maxim learned from an old campaigner at his first blooding: only shoot at what you could see and hit, unless you wanted to scare the pants off somebody you knew was greener than you. And he felt the man above him wasn't.

He pulled the stock of the rifle even tighter into his shoulder, blinked again, hardly daring to breathe. The wood stock of the long gun was warm against his cheek, the barrel he stared down blue-sheened in the morning light.

He blinked once more. Time now seemed to have suspended itself, it moved so slow.

One minute. Two minutes . . .

The sound of a dislodged rock came — then another, this time thirty yards further along the rock line up there. Tightening up more Lateen swung his gaze towards it. The bushwhacker was clearly attempting to work his way around the back of where he *assumed he was.*

Lateen smiled, grimly. Yeah . . . where the bastard assumed he was. That was the big thing here, mister.

He felt sweat run down between the big muscles running down each side of his backbone. Already the morning was warming up. He felt globules of sweat release themselves off his brow, run down to puddle over his eyes before rolling on to his eyelashes and into his eyes.

Annoyed and distracted by them he dashed them away. And to add to his further discomfiture, the scabs on his healing body were beginning to itch like hell, as well as hurt from the salt. He shut the irritations out. He wanted nothing to distract his concentration, not now. He would only have one chance. He knew that, and he had to make that chance good.

For sooner or later that bastard up there would have to expose himself — ease up, look around, when he thought he was safe. And Lateen would have to be ready for him.

But when it happened, it happened quickly. One swift exposure — head and top of the shoulders clear of the skyline — and the man clearly anxious about doing it. But it was enough for Lateen.

He sighted quickly, with skill bred out of an adult life lived depending on his speed and accuracy with a gun to survive. The big rifle boomed into the bright morning, sending the birds squawking into the white sky, the recoil hammering the stock back into his shoulder.

The man's body flung back, arms wide, rifle flying out of his outstretched, clawing right hand. Momentarily, through the sights, Lateen could see the bushwhacker's right eye had become just a round, crimson hole. And as

Lateen jacked in another load he watched the back of the man's skull fly into the blue sky amid a spray of brains and blood, the mess glistening in the morning sun.

The bushwhacker did not make a noise as he collapsed out of view behind the dark, silent rocks.

Without hesitation, knowing the job was done up there, Lateen ran for his horse. If there were more of the bastards he shouldn't be here.

But as he moved he cleared his thinking. No, there couldn't be more. He would have known by now if there was. Then, again, no, he wouldn't. For they do say the one that gets you, you never hear . . .

But it didn't really matter a hoot in hell who the man had been up there, or whether he had friends. The thing was, decided Lateen, *he* was alive and the bushwhacking scum that had been out to get him was dead and he had to move. Maybe he had been a scout sent out from the Double L during the night to probe around, get lucky, come in from another angle . . . whatever, it didn't matter. And, damn it, why did he have to debate things with himself all the time!

Lateen reached his horse and climbed up. Now, he had other, more urgent matters to attend to, for he had exposed his presence. Both the Q Lazy R riders and the men sent out from the Double L now knew that there was somebody else in this neck of the valley. And Lateen also knew, at the moment, he could be a double target on this trigger-happy range. And that didn't sit well at all.

He turned the buckskin round in its own space and put it up the rock-strewn slope towards the top of the broad ridge as fast as its powerful hind quarters could push it.

Near the high crest he pulled his mount to a standstill, just under the skyline. There he dismounted and talked soothingly to the frisky buckskin, who now seemed to have acquired a little of his own anxiety.

There Lateen looked down. Sure enough, the Double L riders had turned and were urging their horses fast towards where he had shot the bushwhacker. The Q Lazy R riders were doing the same thing. Lateen glowered down on the scene. There could be one almighty bust-up when they met.

He pulled out his glass and put it to his eyes and trained it on the Q Lazy R riders. What he saw caused him to snatch the telescope away quickly. Rosemary Francome was at their head, alongside her brother Henry. Several other riders he recognised from his time at the ranch were there also, but the others at the front he didn't know.

He remounted and urged the bay down through the rocks towards the more level valley bottom. He calculated he had two minutes to reach the Q Lazy R riders before the men from the Double L crested the ridge and saw them. What would happen then remained to be seen.

As he broke from the cover of the rocks and turned towards the Q Lazy R men, the riders saw him and pulled their mounts up. He saw Rosemary raise her arm when two or three long guns came up to shoulders.

When Lateen reached them he reined in, his dust drifting on through the grouped riders.

Rosemary was round-eyed, concerned as she met his gaze. "Glen, we heard shots . . ."

Lateen nodded. Quickly he turned to Henry and briefly detailed the attempted bushwhacking and the Double L riders heading their way adding, "I think we ought to get in cover. If I figure it right, there'll be no discussion when they meet you — only with lead. The full story I'll explain later."

A rotund, sour faced man with a star on his chest urged his mount forward. With him came another, steady-eyed man — tall and lean in the saddle.

"You say you've killed a man back there?" the star man said.

Lateen surveyed him with cold eyes. "What you figure I should do — kiss him?"

"Now look here," said the man with the star, red faced. "I'm Clark Fulton, sheriff of this county and I'll take none of that. As for takin' cover, I'll decide on that, too. Now, before I do anythin' I'd like to know what those boys comin' this way have to say. Seems some mighty funny business is goin' on here."

He turned to the tall rider beside him. "And this is deputy U.S. marshal Hiram Jones, investigating the death of Barret Tucker. We're here, mister, to put a final stop to the mayhem goin' on on this range."

From what knowledge he had gathered concerning the attitude of the county law around here, Lateen found himself unimpressed by that statement. But you never knew with county sheriffs, particularly if U.S. marshals were behind them. Votes, and being in good with higher authorities, at the end of the day, talked mighty big.

"Mite late doin' it, ain't you, Sheriff?" he said.

The sheriff's eyes narrowed. "Damn it, what you mean by that? I've had men out here investigatin' — "

The boom of rifles shattered the morning quiet interrupting whatever else Fulton had to say. Dust spat up spurts from around the riders.

The aggression acted like magic on the men. Horses were swung round and spurred, shouts were raised, dust disturbed to form bitter clouds around them. There was an isolated stand of rocks nearby, separated from the ridge. Lateen knew it as Lookout Bluffs. And, as if through unspoken agreement, all riders headed towards it, spreading out amongst the rocks before dismounting to find cover.

Seeing the formidable defences they faced the Double L riders halted just out of gun range. Then a thin, bitter-faced man rode out holding his hand up.

"All we want is Lateen," he bawled. "Send him out and the rest of you can go on your way."

His round, red face now even more sour Sheriff Fulton shouted, "Lookit here, I head the law in this county, boy. You'll have to give me a good reason why for that. I take exception to bein' shot at." Then he broke off, as just realizing the name mentioned. "Lateen you say? What Lateen?"

"The man just rode in to you — Glen Lateen," the Double L rider called. "He's killed his brother Abel, and L. T. Spencer."

Lateen watched Fulton's face lengthen, his handgun come up fast and level. Lateen met the sheriff's hostile, pale stare, peering at him over the gun barrel. Lateen noticed the U.S. deputy marshal's keen gaze was hard on him, too.

Then the sheriff's face scowled. "Well, damn me — the great Glen Lateen," he breathed. The tone sounded sneering. "You've been causin' quite a stir since you came back to this range, mister. Well, L. T. Spencer I ain't about to lose sleep over, but Abel . . . Why, damn it, did you really kill your own brother, boy?"

Rosemary Francome gasped. "Did you, Glen?"

Lateen met Fulton's cold, inquisitive gaze, ignored Rosemary. "No," he said. "But I think I know who did."

"How you know?" This was the deputy U.S. marshal talking. Lateen turned.

"A hard hunch," he said.

A harsh laugh came from Fulton. "That'll stand up in court about as well as a pile o' sand," he said, his scorn clear. His face altered abruptly. "Well, if'n what that man says is right you're just murderin' scum," he breathed. "An' Mr Blackstock is sure goin' to want to see you behind bars. Heard you killed Palau, too. An' I find it odd that Barret Tucker got his soon as you appeared on the range."

Lateen remained calm, watchful; but

he found it was difficult to hold his anger. He nodded towards the strung out Double L riders in front of them, in the distance.

"A moment ago you were talkin' about proof, Sheriff," he said. "Now you're slingin' out all sorts of accusations, as well as insults. Well, I never shot a man in my life that wasn't shootin' back. Now, you ask them boys there how they know I killed Abel. I always understood, there has to be witnesses."

Fulton's thick lips curled in a mocking grin. "I figure your Ma an' Helen wouldn't sanction that bunch on your tail if they weren't one hundred per cent sure."

"You ain't asked them yet," Lateen countered.

"Hell, would they have men after you if they weren't sure?" demanded Fulton. "What I heard, you ain't exactly welcome at the Double L, never have been."

"An' that's proof I killed Abel?" Lateen said. He allowed his gaze to bore into Fulton's. "Well, listen good, Sheriff. Abel's been dead three days. In that time I've been at the Q Lazy R, fit to go nowhere. But speakin' of killin': you asked that scum there who lynched Jim Wayne yet?" He nodded towards the Double L crew.

Rosemary Francome butted in, her pretty face set and pale. "I can swear to Glen bein' at the Q Lazy R," she said.

Fulton swivelled pale eyes on to Rosemary. He looked a little annoyed. "You'll git your chance to speak, li'l lady," he said. He looked at Henry then. "So will you. Just don't you go gittin' so eager. This here man's a known killer."

"Why shouldn't they be eager?" said Lateen. "Somebody has to be. The last law that came to this valley came to the conclusion it was bandits from old Mexico that's been doing the mayhem here in the Mora. Your deputy, so I heard, did some heavy trailing around the saloons of Craddock topin' on free

224

likker before coming to that conclusion and reporting back to the hierarchy at River Falls."

Anger flashed in Fulton's eyes. "Now, look here, Lateen, my deputies are able men and I trust their judgement."

"He wasn't persuaded by Blackstock money, then?" Lateen rapped.

Fulton's face paled. "You're goin' to the edge, boy," he said thinly. He turned to the gaunt-faced man with a longhorn moustache, sitting his horse nearby. He had a sheriff's deputy band around his tall hat. "Put the damned cuffs on him, Jess. He can cool down in Craddock jail while we investigate what's been goin' on in this valley."

By the time Fulton returned his gaze, Lateen had stroked out his Colt with blurring speed. His glare over the gunmetal was icy and direct and on the bulky sheriff. The U.S. marshal sat square-faced and narrow-eyed, clearly impressed by the swiftness of the draw.

But he did say, with urgency, "Think

about it first, Lateen," his tone neutral. Clearly this man didn't pick culprits until he was sure of the ground he stood on, even if they were known mankillers.

Lateen nodded but kept his gaze on the sheriff. "I always do," he said. He eyed Fulton. "Now, understand this, Sheriff, you ain't putting me anywhere. I'm inclined to believe the trouble in this valley, so far as I can make out, is Lateen trouble, aided by a silk-tongued Horst Blackstock who has had his killings done by L. T. Spencer. And in one of those killin's I include Abel. But that won't occur any more. Spencer thought he could rub me out last night. He didn't manage it. Don't make the same mistake. Now, as the last remaining male Lateen, but wanting to be shut of this range, I intend only one thing before I go: put what troubles this range right."

Hearing that, a shot came from the Double L rider, cutting off any further words. Lateen felt lead fan past his face then heard Fulton grunt with pain and sag in the saddle.

Lateen whirled round and levelled his gun at the shootist. Already the Double L rider was in a flat-out run, yelling and heading for the line of riders standing off from the group of rocks.

He sent three shots after him, but it was too great a range for a handgun.

As he did deputy U.S. marshal Hiram Jones bellowed, "That does it, men. Get to your saddles. Miss Rosemary, see to Sheriff Fulton if you please."

There was but a moment's hesitation before men went for horses and mounted.

Lateen stared at Jones, delaying him with a hand on his arm. "Marshal, much as I'd like to join you, I got business to settle at the Double L."

Jones narrowed his eyes, hesitated a moment as if debating the legality of the situation, then he said, "You're your own man, I guess. But you are still included in our investigations, Lateen."

Lateen eyed the marshal levelly. "Well, I can live with that. But I think I know who killed Barret Tucker, deputy. L. T. Spencer, on Horst Blackstock's instructions. Barret was asking too many questions."

"If you can get me proof of that — "

Lateen mounted his buckskin. "I'll do my damnedest."

Soon the sheriff's men and the riders from the Q Lazy R were forming up, waiting for Hiram Jones' instructions.

Jones pulled down at his brown stetson, his square face grim. "Right boys, let's run 'em to hell an' gone. Those who resist arrest when called — shoot them down like dogs."

As the posse rode off Lateen looked down at Rosemary Francome. She was looking at Fulton's wound caringly.

"I'll be back as soon as I can, Rosemary," he said. "Think you can manage?"

"I can manage, Glen," she said. "I brought bandages an' stuff, just in case."

From the ground Sheriff Fulton growled. "I'll be all right. I'm trustin' you to haul up the sonsofbitches who ordered this done to me, Lateen."

Lateen smiled wryly. "I figure it was for me," he said. "But how about Jim Wayne an' Barret Tucker? Don't they figure in this, too?"

Fulton scowled impatiently. "Damn it, you know what I mean."

Yeah, thought Lateen. Sure I do. County Sheriff Fulton has seen the way the wind blows.

He swung the buckskin round and urged it towards the Double L, Blackstock and Helen.

14

WHEN he pulled the buckskin
to a halt outside the mansion
that was the Double L ranchhouse in a cloud of dust, Lateen
bawled,

"Helen!"

A few ranchhands were working
about the place. They heeded him
little. They were the work force of
the Double L. They would be here
when the border scum were killed or
run out of the country.

But they did look up with curious
eyes.

Helen came to the door. Her oval,
beautiful face was pale. By her side was
the dark-haired woman: Palau's widow.
Ma was nowhere to be seen.

"Glen," Helen said flatly. There was
no false enthusiasm. Nothing, only
tension and cold resentment, perhaps

a little curiosity.

"Heard what you had to say last night, Helen," he said. "About not bein' kin, about wantin' the ranch, wantin' to kill me."

Her stare was level, iron-grey like his own.

"Then you heard enough," she said.

"We could have worked somethin' out about the ranch, if you had told me," he said. "You're still precious to me."

Helen laughed hollowly. "Precious? You're only precious to yourself, Glen Lateen. If I meant so much to you, you would have stayed on when you came back from the war. If you had, things would have been different."

"Blackstock's blinded you, Helen," he said. "But there's still time, maybe, to pull back."

"Horst loves me," she barked. "Do you? Did you love me when you ran away?" She looked down, whispered, "I always knew I loved you, Glen, but never as a sister. I should have guessed then — realized. Can you imagine how hard that was, feeling like that and not not . . . being . . . able to . . . ?"

Her gaze went distant, as if she was remembering — way back. Then she said, "Well, last year, as you know, I learnt why. Not kin, she said."

Lateen felt as though his heart had again become lead within him. "The past can't be brought back, Helen, an' I gotta ask: Did you kill Abel?"

Her stare went icy, kind of mad-looking, before it filled with pain. "He was going to tell it all," she said. Her voice became whining. "He got stinking drunk again. He'd been listening at keyholes, like you. I followed him up to the hideout. He was going to tell you, tell Sheriff Fulton — tell Ma — tell . . ."

Helen's voice trailed off. She didn't look well. She was pale and stare-eyed.

"You're sick, Helen," Lateen said.

"But *I* ain't, Glen." The voice came from behind him.

Lateen whirled. Blackstock was standing by the barn, maybe fifty yards away. He had a rifle on the crook of his arm.

From where he was, the chance of hitting Blackstock was very slim with a short barrelled Colt Frontier. It had to be the rifle, in the saddle scabbard. And the chances of getting that into play was . . .

Lateen stared with steel-grey eyes.

"You kill Barret Tucker?" he demanded.

Blackstock laughed, his bluff face bunching at the cheeks. "You think I'm a fool?" he said. "I had L. T. Spencer do it. Barret was getting more than halfway to the truth."

"An' Jim Wayne? L.T. as well?"

Blackstock shrugged. "He could get over-enthusiastic. A trait I intended to rectify when his usefulness was over."

Lateen's grim face lengthened. "You bastard," he growled. "You've come a long way since Genner's Ford."

Blackstock's face lost its grin. "How

you know about that, Lateen?"

"I was there."

At that Blackstock moved, bringing up the rifle, but Lateen was moving, too. His hand was grabbing the Winchester. He was dropping out of the saddle, levering a shell into the breech as he did.

He fired from the hip. He could see Blackstock was sighting on him. But not quickly enough.

Lateen saw his load hit Blackstock's shoulder, spinning him round just as he fired.

And behind him, Lateen heard Helen gasp, then cry out. And Lateen found himself torn — torn between his concern for Helen or watching Blackstock.

Blackstock won and he could see the man was lining up to fire again when Lateen watched him falter. Now Blackstock was staring past him, to where Lateen knew Helen had been standing on the terrace.

Then Blackstock gave an animal

cry, dropped his rifle and run to her though he was bleeding heavily from his wound.

Lateen stepped aside, but followed him with his pointed gun.

He saw Helen was lying on the terrace. Blood soaked her pink silk dress at the front. Palau's wife was standing by her side screaming, her hand to her mouth, looking down at her.

His anguished cries tearing from him Blackstock went to his knees, drew Helen's limp form to him. "Helen! For God's sake, Helen! Oh, my dear, dear Helen!"

Lateen stood, not knowing what to do. Helen must have been hit by Blackstock's bullet. What crazy madness it all was.

Now Blackstock's heavy sobs sounded across the dry packed ground. He had clearly forgotten everything around him. Lateen could see the man was completely overwrought.

Lateen didn't know what to do with

his hands, his mind, anything. He was witnessing what he would maybe feel had he himself done this to his own love, Mary Gullet. He, too, would maybe have gone crazy with grief.

He realized Blackstock was now turning on him, staring at him. And he had a derringer in his hand. "You, Lateen! You! A womankiller now."

And oddly all Lateen found he could do was look stupefied at the small gun, stunned as he was by Helen's shooting.

Even when he did react, he knew he was bringing the Winchester up far too late.

But the blast from the shotgun behind sent Blackstock lurching forward, as if propelled by a powerful force. When he hit the dirt Lateen could see the big hole in his back, the blood pumping out of it. And he was dead.

Stunned he looked up. Ma was standing in the frame of the doorway, smoking shotgun in her hand.

She stared for long moments at the

body, then at Helen, now quiet and limp on the terrace. Blackstock's niece still was standing, screaming.

Then Ma stepped forward, her face a mask — white and frozen. She smacked the woman hard across her face, cutting off her hysterics like a tap cuts off water.

Then it was deathly quiet, gunsmoke drifting across the space between the house and the nearby barn.

Then Ma said, "I heard it all, Glen. May God despise Helen for what she done."

Then Lateen came back, came rational again.

He shook his head. "No, Ma, I can't see it quite like that. I'll never be able to."

He turned and walked stiffly towards his horse.

"Where are you going?" his mother demanded.

"I got folks in Wyoming I'm longin' to see," he said mechanically.

"What about the Double L?" she

demanded harshly. "What about here? You're the last of the clan. You've got to stay."

Lateen turned and levelled his gaze to meet his Ma's cold stare. "No, Ma," he said. "Helen loved the Double L — loved you, though you'd no eyes to see it. Give it to little James. She would have liked that. That's what she had come to want."

His mother's voice was now stark on the cool morning air. "I'm dyin', Glen," she shrilled. "The boy's too young."

"Put a manager in," said Lateen. "The boy can come with me. I'll oversee the ranch 'til he comes of age."

"It's too thin," Ma said.

Her voice was harsh with regret, despair — as though echoing back, down through the years.

Lateen shrugged. "It's all I can give to say sorry to Helen."

"Helen?" His mother spat the words. "She killed your brother. What about me — you ever said sorry to me?"

Lateen stared at his mother's crying face.

"No, Ma, I never have," he said. "Maybe I should have done."

Lateen climbed up on to the buckskin, turned it off towards the ridge to find Rosemary Francome.

Then he would ride to Wyoming, to Mary Gullet and peace. He'd take the boy, too, if Ma had the mind to heed him.

THE END

FIGHTING RAMROD
Charles N. Heckelmann

Most men would have cut their losses, but Frazer counted the bullets in his guns and said he'd soak the range in blood before he'd give up another inch of what was his.

LONE GUN
Eric Allen

Smoke Blackbird had been away too long. The Lequires had seized the Blackbird farm, forcing the Indians and settlers off, and no one seemed willing to fight! He had to fight alone.

THE THIRD RIDER
Barry Cord

Mel Rawlins wasn't going to let anything stand in his way. His father was murdered, his two brothers gone. Now Mel rode for vengeance.

ARIZONA DRIFTERS
W. C. Tuttle

When drifting Dutton and Lonnie Steelman decide to become partners they find that they have a common enemy in the formidable Thurston brothers.

TOMBSTONE
Matt Braun

Wells Fargo paid Luke Starbuck to outgun the silver-thieving stagecoach gang at Tombstone. Before long Luke can see the only thing bearing fruit in this eldorado will be the gallows tree.

HIGH BORDER RIDERS
Lee Floren

Buckshot McKee and Tortilla Joe cut the trail of a border tough who was running Mexican beef into Texas. They stopped the smuggler in his tracks.

BRETT RANDALL, GAMBLER
E. B. Mann

Larry Day had the choice of running away from the law or of assuming a dead man's place. No matter what he decided he was bound to end up dead.

THE GUNSHARP
William R. Cox

The Eggerleys weren't very smart. They trained their sights on Will Carney and Arizona's biggest blood bath began.

THE DEPUTY OF SAN RIANO
Lawrence A. Keating and
Al. P. Nelson

When a man fell dead from his horse, Ed Grant was spotted riding away from the scene. The deputy sheriff rode out after him and came up against everything from gunfire to dynamite.

FARGO: MASSACRE RIVER
John Benteen

The ambushers up ahead had now blocked the road. Fargo's convoy was a jumble, a perfect target for the insurgents' weapons!

SUNDANCE: DEATH IN THE LAVA
John Benteen

The Modoc's captured the wagon train and its cargo of gold. But now the halfbreed they called Sundance was going after it . . .

HARSH RECKONING
Phil Ketchum

Five years of keeping himself alive in a brutal prison had made Brand tough and careless about who he gunned down . . .

FARGO: PANAMA GOLD
John Benteen

With foreign money behind him, Buckner was going to destroy the Panama Canal before it could be completed. Fargo's job was to stop Buckner.

FARGO:
THE SHARPSHOOTERS
John Benteen

The Canfield clan, thirty strong were raising hell in Texas. Fargo was tough enough to hold his own against the whole clan.

PISTOL LAW
Paul Evan Lehman

Lance Jones came back to Mustang for just one thing — revenge! Revenge on the people who had him thrown in jail.

HELL RIDERS
Steve Mensing

Wade Walker's kid brother, Duane, was locked up in the Silver City jail facing a rope at dawn. Wade was a ruthless outlaw, but he was smart, and he had vowed to have his brother out of jail before morning!

DESERT OF THE DAMNED
Nelson Nye

The law was after him for the murder of a marshal — a murder he didn't commit. Breen was after him for revenge — and Breen wouldn't stop at anything . . . blackmail, a frameup . . . or murder.

DAY OF THE COMANCHEROS
Steven C. Lawrence

Their very name struck terror into men's hearts — the Comancheros, a savage army of cutthroats who swept across Texas, leaving behind a bloodstained trail of robbery and murder.

SUNDANCE: SILENT ENEMY
John Benteen

A lone crazed Cheyenne was on a personal war path. They needed to pit one man against one crazed Indian. That man was Sundance.

LASSITER
Jack Slade

Lassiter wasn't the kind of man to listen to reason. Cross him once and he'll hold a grudge for years to come — if he let you live that long.

LAST STAGE TO GOMORRAH
Barry Cord

Jeff Carter, tough ex-riverboat gambler, now had himself a horse ranch that kept him free from gunfights and card games. Until Sturvesant of Wells Fargo showed up.

McALLISTER ON THE COMANCHE CROSSING
Matt Chisholm

The Comanche, McAllister owes them a life — and the trail is soaked with the blood of the men who had tried to outrun them before.

QUICK-TRIGGER COUNTRY
Clem Colt

Turkey Red hooked up with Curly Bill Graham's outlaw crew. But wholesale murder was out of Turk's line, so when range war flared he bucked the whole border gang alone . . .

CAMPAIGNING
Jim Miller

Ambushed on the Santa Fe trail, Sean Callahan is saved by two Indian strangers. But there'll be more lead and arrows flying before the band join Kit Carson against the Comanches.

GUNSLINGER'S RANGE
Jackson Cole

Three escaped convicts are out for revenge. They won't rest until they put a bullet through the head of the dirty snake who locked them behind bars.

RUSTLER'S TRAIL
Lee Floren

Jim Carlin knew he would have to stand up and fight because he had staked his claim right in the middle of Big Ike Outland's best grass.

THE TRUTH ABOUT SNAKE RIDGE
Marshall Grover

The troubleshooters came to San Cristobal to help the needy. For Larry and Stretch the turmoil began with a brawl and then an ambush.

WOLF DOG RANGE
Lee Floren

Will Ardery would stop at nothing, unless something stopped him first — like a bullet from Pete Manly's gun.

DEVIL'S DINERO
Marshall Grover

Plagued by remorse, a rich old reprobate hired the Texas Trouble-shooters to deliver a fortune in greenbacks to each of his victims.

GUNS OF FURY
Ernest Haycox

Dane Starr, alias Dan Smith, wanted to close the door on his past and hang up his guns, but people wouldn't let him.